# A VERY MERRY MATCH POINT

A Why Choose Christmas Novella

ANASTASIJA WHITE

This book is a work of fiction. Names, characters, locales, businesses, events and incidents are products of the author's imagination or are used fictitiously. Any resemblance to actual person, living or dead; events; or locations is entirely coincidental.

The author acknowledges the trademark status and trademark owners of various products, and/or brands referenced in the work of fiction. The publication/use of these trademarks is not authorized, associated with, or sponsored by the trademark owners.

Line Editing: Beth, VB Edits, https://vbeditsromance.com/

Edited by Caroline Knecht, https://reedsy.com/caroline-knecht

Edited by Lawrence Editing, https://www.lawrenceediting.com/

Characters arts and Cover Design by Anna Silka, https://www.instagram.com/silka.art/

Characters arts by Alina Alilyushka, https://www.instagram.com/alilyushka/

Characters art by Darya, https://www.instagram.com/darya.mist.art/

Characters art by xenychan, https://www.instagram.com/xenychan/

This book is intended for an 18+ audience.

For trigger warnings, please visit https://shor.by/AVMMP

ISBN 978-609-08-1018-7 (ebook)

ISBN 978-609-08-1017-0 (paperback)

*To the ones who learned to protect their hearts, yet still feel deeply and choose love even when it scares them.*

*And to the readers who (secretly or not) want to be worshipped, adored, and thoroughly ruined by two hot hockey players...I wrote this one for you.*

*Каханне прыходзіць рэдка, але назаўсёды*[1].

1. Love doesn't come often, but stays forever

# Playlist

"Last Christmas" - Wham!
"Love In The Dark" - Adele
"We Found Love" - Rihanna feat. Calvin Harris
"Christmas Tree Farm" - Taylor Swift
"Dying To Love" - Bad Omens
"Love You Like A Love Song" - Selena Gomez & The Scene
"Snowman - Sia
"Just the Way You Are" - Bruno Mars
"Perfect" - Ed Sheeran
"Euclid" - Sleep Token

Find the rest of **A Very Merry Match Point** playlist here:

# Author's Note

*Dear readers,*

THANK YOU for your desire to read **A Very Merry Match Point (AVMMP)**! It's my first ever novella, very first insta-love story, and very very first why-choose romance. I had a lot of fun working on it, and I can't wait to know what YOU think.

This book contains the following warnings: alcohol consumption, explicit language, mention of death of a parent and of a family member, on-page sexual content between two / three consenting adults, slight kink exploration.

Also, please keep in mind that Yana is an Eastern European girl, she's a Slavic girl with a black cat energy. She doesn't fold easily even when she's attracted to someone :), but once she learns she can trust this person? She will do anything for them.

Really hope you will enjoy this one.

*With love,*
*Ana.*

# ONE

## No Hockey Players

YANA

"THE MOMENT ROSIE TOLD ME SHE SAW THE GUYS FROM the California Thunders here, I knew we had to try it," Chloe says as she pushes open the passenger door.

"I still don't get the appeal," I mutter, climbing out of the car.

Lips twisted, she narrows her hazel eyes at me. "Don't you know a guy from the team? Rowan?"

"Roman," I correct her.

"Semantics. What's important here is that you know one of them. If we're lucky and they're here tonight, you can introduce me." Winking, she tucks a strand of her dark brown hair behind her ear. "Ready to go?"

"Yeah." I force a small smile and take in the packed parking lot.

"Great."

I round the car and head to the steakhouse. Twinkling Christmas lights strung up between palm trees light up the street, a California kind of festive.

Chloe links her arm with mine, chatting about the details her colleague gave her about this new place.

I listen half-heartedly, enjoying the slight bite of the winter air. The December wind slips beneath my unbuttoned black wrap coat and beige cashmere sweater, a little reminder of the upcoming holidays.

I visited my family in Belarus a few Christmases ago, and though it was colder there than it is here, at least there was snow.

Ugh, I can't wait for my solo trip to Lake Tahoe. To spend a few days in a cabin in the woods, enjoying the fresh snow. It's exactly what I need before I leave for Australia.

Chloe mentions her mom and how she helped her get ready for dinner via FaceTime, but my brain is elsewhere. It always is these days. But I don't talk about it with her. I don't talk about it with anyone outside my team and my parents. It's easier to keep my shit locked inside.

I should've been in Doha in November, walking onto the court at the WTA Finals. One of the top eight players in the world. A dream I'd worked my whole life for. But I pulled out.

Officially, my team blamed tendonitis.

And my wrist really was a mess.

But *I* was a mess too. Burned out, running on empty, spiraling. And no one outside my team noticed. My friends continued to fixate on parties and outfits and the guys they were into at any given moment.

Normally, I'd appreciate the distraction from constant training, playing, and competing.

But after I dropped out from Doha, I went quiet. Still, only my family asked what was going on.

Distancing myself was my response. This is the first time I've been out since, and with how easily I get irritated, I'm afraid I made a mistake.

It's embarrassing to admit that six months post-breakup, I'm still struggling to come to terms with it. I'm twenty-four. It's time to grow up and move on. Though maybe I can't get over it because of how it happened. Being cheated on in one's apartment—in one's own bed—is a humbling experience.

"Are you even listening to me?" Chloe asks, her pitch so startling it makes me stagger.

I shake my head and fix my focus on her. "Sorry. Spaced out for a minute."

She stops a few feet away from the restaurant's entrance, a little frown etched onto her face, her eyes holding mine. "Are you okay? I didn't want to bug you while I was in Singapore, but now I regret not asking about why you dropped out of the WTA tournament."

I force a smile, my lips trembling. There's a reason I said yes to her dinner invitation. Out of all my close friends in the US, I enjoy Chloe's company the most. Plus, she reminds me of my childhood best friend, Karina, who still lives in Belarus.

Chloe is my favorite person here. I need to act like it because she doesn't deserve my moodiness.

"I've been better." I shrug. "But I'm okay. I've got some time off so I can get ready for the Australian Open."

Physically? I'm ready. Mentally? Not even close. The anxiety that settled in the pit of my stomach after I walked in on Eddie with his mistress has yet to fade. Neither has the shame. Even with the help of my therapist, Dr. Lloyd, I have a long way to go.

During our last session, she made a very good point. She said, "I know you feel ashamed, but I want you to pause for a moment and ask yourself what *you* did wrong. You trusted someone. You let him into your life and your home. That isn't weakness or foolishness. The shame doesn't belong to you, only to the person who broke your heart."

Even so, I can't shake the shame that comes with the realization that I didn't notice the signs. And I can't stop asking myself questions like "What if I were different?" or "What if I had more free time?"

"Yana?" Chloe's soft voice pulls me back to reality.

I refocus on her and take a deep breath. "Sorry. I don't want to ruin your night. Lately, it feels like that's all I do."

"Stop it." She tugs on my arm. "I love you, girl. I'm here for you, no matter what. And"—she waggles her brows—"you couldn't ruin my night...unless you refused to introduce me to your hockey friend."

I shake my head. "You're impossible. Roman is married, with a daughter."

With a wicked smile, she points at me. "I know, but I also know he has a bunch of lonely, single teammates."

A burst of laughter escapes me. "Babe, we're talking about hockey players. *NHL*-level players. These guys are never lonely, trust me."

"Stop being a spoilsport." She pouts, her bottom lip stuck out. "Sue me for wanting something fun. Or maybe something serious. You never know what surprises life has in store for you."

I let out a little huff. "With my luck? I'm fucking terrified of life's surprises."

"Shush. Let's go inside." She shivers. "It's getting colder."

The second we step through the heavy glass doors, the warmth of the restaurant washes away the December chill. The air smells like steak and garlic and butter, rich and mouthwatering, mixed with the faint sweetness of wine. Laughter and the sound of clinking glasses bounce off dark wood panels and leather booths. Low-hanging lights glow golden over polished tables. The atmosphere is pleasant and intimate.

I can see why this place is popular.

A young woman with a sleek high ponytail and a black dress greets us at the hostess stand, checking the reservation once Chloe gives her the details. With a nod and a practiced smile, she shows us to our table.

"Oh my God." My friend tugs on the sleeve of my coat as we follow the hostess. "They're here."

She's right. Though the place is packed with couples and even several families, with servers in black weaving through the crowd carrying trays of cocktails and delicious-looking dishes, the California Thunders make their presence known. Loud chatter and cheers spread through the room like waves crashing onto the shore.

"Do you see your friend?" Chloe asks.

"Not yet." I catch my bottom lip between my teeth as I discreetly survey the men. "And I'm not sure I will. Roma[1] is a family guy."

---

1. A short version of the name Roman

"Fingers crossed he is." She bumps her hip into mine. "But if not, at least we're in for a good meal."

I chuckle. "Love the enthusiasm."

Our table is near the hockey team's, and their laughter is loud. I scrunch my nose. I don't love when people act as if they're alone in a public space.

When the server approaches, I order the filet mignon with baked potatoes and a sparkling water with lemon and mint. Chloe orders a rib eye with creamed spinach and a Cosmo.

"How was your business trip?" I ask, leaning back into my chair.

"It was good. Singapore is beautiful. Lively. And the people there are nice, but I was so busy that I barely had time to go out and explore."

"You were there for a month, and you didn't have time to explore?"

She sighs dramatically. "Not at all."

"Aww, poor thing. Maybe next time you're there, you'll have more time—"

"Don't jinx me," she hisses. "Next time, they better send Silvia instead. I missed my bed, and especially Billy. I've been so busy since I got back that I haven't even had time to pick up my dog. I miss him terribly."

I chuckle. Her toy poodle is the cutest. "I bet he's having the time of his life at your mom's."

"He gained almost seven pounds while I was away! I'm afraid I won't recognize him."

"You're so dramatic." I shake my head. "You should've been an actress, not a project manager for an IT company."

She opens her mouth to speak, but the buzz of her phone stops her. As she checks her messages, I scan the restaurant. Several people sit at the bar, some alone, sipping on drinks. The majority of the crowd is made up of couples, and a handful of families are seated nearby too.

When a little boy with curly hair catches my eye and waves at me, warmth blooms inside me, and a smile curves my lips.

A prickling sensation at the back of my neck sends goosebumps all over my body. Like a little spark sliding under my skin and making it burn.

Brows knit, I continue my perusal, this time searching for the person who's watching me.

Eventually, a pair of crystal blue eyes snags my attention. The man, one of the hockey players nearby, has dark hair and pale skin, making his eye color pop. His cheekbones are sharp and covered in a slight stubble, and his lips are full, as if they were made for smirking. And the smirk he's flashing me is dangerous. His hair is messy on top but shaved on the sides, giving him a just-rolled-out-of-bed look. Add in the way his white shirt hugs the broad plane of his chest so perfectly, and it's clear that he's trouble.

That alone is enough to force me to tear my gaze away from him.

When I do, I catch sight of Roman Pashkevich, the Thunders' right defenseman. He's a fellow Belarusian I met a few years ago, right after I moved to California. The guy is the sweetest, though his wife, Nevaeh, swears that most of the world doesn't see the softer side of him. Apparently, he only acts like that with people he cares about. I don't know how I ended up on that list, but I'm not complaining. I love him and his family.

"I see Roman," I say.

Eyes snapping to me, Chloe straightens. "Really? Will you talk to him? Ask him if he'll introduce me to the guys?"

"Is this a line item on some kind of weird bucket list I don't know about? First you were searching for a baseball player, then it was basketball. Now hockey."

"Different guys, different flavors." She winks at me.

I pretend to gag, and it only makes her laugh.

"Go," she urges me. "While you chat them up, I need to check my email. My boss has clearly forgotten that my workday is over."

I stand and slowly head to the Thunders' table.

Roman turns when I'm a few feet away and breaks into a warm smile.

"*Privet! Kakimi sud'bami?*[2]" He scoops me into his arms and presses me to his chest. Then he leans away, his deep turquoise eyes fixed on me. "*Ochen' zhal' naschet turnira. Nev i ya tak zhdali ego. Hoteli za tebya pobolet' kak obychno*[3]."

"*Podruga vernulas' s komandirovki, i pozvala menya na uzhin. Reshila soglasit'sya. Skol'ko mozhno uzhe handrit'?*[4]" I give him a smile and step back. "*A naschet turnira—budet sleduyushyi v sleduyushem godu. Mozhet togda povezet*[5]."

"*Kogda ty na korte, ty neveroyatnaya. Povezet obyazatel'no*[6]."

Heart full, I say, "*Spasibo*[7], *Rom*[8]."

Warmth courses through my veins, making me feel weightless. He's six years older than me, and he's always treated me like his little sister. I adore him like I would a brother. But truthfully, I keep up with Nevaeh more than Roman.

When he leans in and whispers that Nevaeh is pregnant again, I feign surprise and give him a quick hug. There's no way I'll admit that his wife spilled the beans just before I was set to leave for Doha.

Roman and I chat, and the conversation is easy, grounding. It feels good to just talk, to not have to perform.

I smile, my posture relaxed. That is, until a voice cuts in, snagging our attention.

The man's tone is low, his voice a lazy drawl. "We're in America. Maybe switch to English so the rest of us don't feel left out?"

What the hell?

Annoyed, I turn toward the source of the shitty comment, and I'm instantly met with familiar crystal blue eyes and that smirk.

---

2. Hi! What are you doing here?
3. I'm very sorry about the tournament. Nev and I were very excited about it. Wanted to root for you as we always do.
4. My friend is back from her business trip; and she invited me to dinner. I decided to agree. For how long can I be moody?
5. As for the tournament—there will be another one next year. Maybe I'll be lucky then.
6. When you're on court, you're incredible. You will be lucky, I'm sure.
7. Thank you
8. Rom is a short version of a short version Roma of the name Roman

"What's your problem?" I ask the disgustingly good-looking man.

"My problem? You're speaking a language I don't understand. For all I know, you're insulting the rest of us," he taunts, clearly pleased with himself and his bullshit.

I frown. "Do you really have such little faith in your teammate?" He sobers quickly, and the reaction is priceless, but I don't back down. "You think he'd be insulting you behind your back?"

"Yeah, Hayes," Roman chimes in with his arms crossed over his chest. "I'd love to hear the answer to that too."

Jaw clenched, Hayes glares at me. When he focuses on Roman again, his features soften. "Sorry, man. I was just trying to tease your friend. Clearly, the joke didn't land. You know I respect you. It wasn't a jab at you in any way."

"Do better next time," Roman grunts. "There are a thousand ways to get a girl's attention without insulting her."

Hayes huffs. "Her attention is the last thing I want."

I shouldn't care about the words that leave this asshole's mouth, but the comment hits too close to home.

"Just like *I* don't want yours," I state. "The next time you're eavesdropping, you'll know you're being insulted when you hear '*Idi na huyi*,' since that means 'go fuck yourself.' Have a nice day."

The whole table bursts into laughter.

I'm biting my bottom lip, fighting a grin, when I lock eyes with the guy sitting beside Hayes. I swear this man walked straight out of a surf ad. He's all sun and waves. Blond hair that refuses to stay put, sun-kissed skin, and honeyed brown eyes. He's huge. Way bigger than Hayes, who's on the leaner side. Broad shoulders, muscular chest, the kind of bulk that belongs in a weight room.

The feature that catches my attention, though, is his genuine smile.

Goodness. What am I doing?

I blink, cutting eye contact, and sneak a glance at Hayes. His cheeks are red, and he's chewing on the inside of his bottom lip, staring straight ahead.

The blond beside him continues assessing me.

I peer over my shoulder, checking on Chloe. She's still at our table, her focus fixed on her phone screen. I return to my conversation with Roman, asking if he'd mind introducing her to the team later, and he agrees.

When I get back to the table, I discover our meals have already arrived. As I hover beside my chair, my skin tingles, and my pulse picks up. Once again, someone is watching. As I lower into my seat, I peek over my shoulder. Sure enough, I find eyes on me. But not just one set.

Not only is the handsome blond looking at me, but so is Hayes.

They couldn't look more different, yet each is gorgeous in his own right. Their attention makes my heart skip and my cheeks warm. When my pussy flutters too, I know I'm in trouble. I leave for Tahoe in two weeks, where I plan to hide away in a cabin in the woods so I can get my mind right for Australia. No distractions. No detours. And definitely no hockey players.

At least that's what I tell myself.

TWO

# I Want to Ask Her Out

LOGAN

HAYES FUMES AS THE REDHEAD WANDERS AWAY. I, ON THE other hand, hold back a laugh. He's my best friend, but he deserved to be put in his place after the disrespect he showed her. Her conversation with Roman was none of his business.

Though I can't say I'm not curious about her.

I eye Roman. "Who was that?"

He puts his device down and meets my gaze. "A friend."

"You don't recognize her?" Colton Thompson, the team's center and our captain, asks. His knowing smile tells me I'm missing something, but I've genuinely never seen that woman before.

"No. Should I?"

Drake Benson, our right winger, laughs. "Guy clearly knows nothing about tennis."

I assess each of the guys, frowning. "She's...a tennis player?"

"Yup." Roman nods. "One of the best. She's ranked in the top ten of the Women's Tennis Association."

"Wow. I had no clue." I tilt my head to the side. "How do you know her?"

Roman scratches his brow. "I met Yana when she moved to Santa Clara, four years ago, maybe? She's from Belarus, like me, and we hit it off quickly. Being so far from home, it's good to have a friend from a similar background. We can reminisce about the places we loved to visit when we were younger. That kind of thing."

"I get it." I drape my arm around Hayes's shoulder, startling him. "Camden and I have been best friends since preschool. Even the years we spent apart in college, and later in the NHL, didn't dampen our friendship."

"You're such a sap," Camden grunts. He pushes me away and zeroes in on Roman. "And I'm sorry for what I said. I didn't mean to offend you. All I wanted was to rile that girl up a little."

"Forget about it. We're cool." Roman smirks. "Yana taught you a good lesson."

From there, the conversation turns to other topics. At first, I try to listen, but I quickly find myself staring at the woman—Yana—again. She's sitting at a table not far from ours, with a brunette across from her. The joy radiating from her as they talk and laugh only makes me smile wider.

Damn, she's stunning.

Her face is the kind a man doesn't forget. Big round eyes framed by long dark lashes. The light in the restaurant is dim, but her eyes look like they are a unique gray-green color. Her high cheekbones sharpen her beauty, though they're in juxtaposition to the light dusting of freckles across the bridge of her nose and the fullness of her lips. Her nearly porcelain skin only makes her freckles stand out more. She's warm and magnetic, making it nearly impossible to take my eyes off her.

I want to ask her out.

"Are you talking to yourself?" Camden asks, breaking the spell I've been under.

Confused, I peer over at him. "What?"

"You just said, 'I want to ask her out.'"

My jaw unhinges. I did?

Brows pulled together, he studies me. "Were you talking about that redhead?"

"Technically, I've been thinking about her." I flash him a smile.

He rolls his eyes. "You're fucking weird. She's so full of herself."

My smile drops, and an unfamiliar protectiveness flares to life in my veins. "What makes you say that?"

"Didn't you see how she snapped at me? Attitude for days."

I hold his gaze, leaning forward. "It's not an attitude. It's her protecting her boundaries and putting you in your place. And saying she's so full of herself? There's no need for that kind of shit. You shouldn't be talking about women like that, especially around me. You may be my best friend, but I won't put up with it."

"Whatever." He picks up his glass of whiskey and downs it in one go. "I'm ready to leave."

I take a sip of my own drink and set the glass down easily. "Bored already?"

He grimaces. "When Jones invited us out for his birthday, I expected a club or a private party. Not this dinner at a fancy steakhouse."

"It's only a surprise for you since this is your first season on the team. Now you know Jones hates clubs and parties. The fact that he even organized a dinner is surprising, really."

"Okay." He roughs a hand down his face. "Think I pissed off Pashkevich? I like the guy, and I don't want to fuck up the team's vibe."

"Relax. If Roman says you're good, he means it. He's always honest, even when it makes you uncomfortable."

"As if replacing Clay Rodgers isn't stressful enough." He looks up at the ceiling. "Trying to live up to his legacy while being surrounded by his best friends keeps me constantly on edge."

"You need to get laid."

Glaring, he pushes himself away from the table. "What fucking wonderful advice from my best friend."

Hands deep in his pockets and shoulders tense, he strides toward the restroom. Shit. I should've kept my mouth shut. Next week is the second anniversary of his granny's death, and since she raised him after his parents died, it's gotta be hard on him. And I just acted like a total douche.

Wanting to help him but unsure how, I turn to where he stormed off. Should I go after him?

Turns out I don't need to. He's still in the dining area, and he's staring at Yana.

And fuck. She's staring right back at him, and I swear I can almost see sparks flying between them.

Hell no.

I have to ask her out first.

YANA and the brunette wander over to our table a while later, both wearing winter coats. She puts her hand on Roman's shoulder, snagging his attention.

"We're leaving. Just wanted to say bye."

Roman stands and wraps her in a quick side hug. "It was nice to see you. You should stop by next week. Nev will be ecstatic, and so will Diana."

"I just might do that. I haven't seen your girls in a while. I miss them." She smiles up at him. The expression drops quickly, though, and she slaps her forehead. "*Bozhe*[1], where are my manners? Roman, this is Chloe."

"It's nice to meet you, Chloe." Roman gives her a hug as well and turns back to the table. "I apparently lack manners too. Guys, this is my friend Yana." He points at her. "And this is her friend Chloe."

The guys all greet them politely, a chorus of hellos.

Yana nods, but Chloe breaks into a dazzling smile. "I'm so happy to meet y'all. The Thunders are my favorite team, and it's such a pleasure to watch you play."

The group breaks into a round of thank-yous, and the table falls into silence.

Yana peeks over at her friend, who's wearing a frown, probably

1. God

surprised by such an unenthusiastic response. Chloe is gorgeous, after all—though not nearly as beautiful as Yana. Our ambivalence isn't personal. We came straight from practice, and we've been here for a few hours. What we all want is to go home, no matter how tempting the girl is.

"We better go." Yana loops her arm through her friend's. "*Poka*[2], Roma." She surveys the table, her attention lingering on Camden and then landing on me. "Bye, boys."

"Bye."

As the girls walk away, I tap my fingers on the table, considering my next move. Beside me, Camden shifts. The subtle move sends me into action.

It's probably shitty of me, but I really want a chance with Yana. And after their argument, I don't think my best friend will ask her out anyway. Hell, he probably isn't even into her. Even so...

"I'll be back," I mutter, jumping to my feet.

I weave through the crowd and hurry out of the restaurant. On the sidewalk, it takes a moment to find the women, but when I do, I jog toward them.

*Make it or break it, Logan.*

"Yana!" I call.

She glances over her shoulder, her brows knit. Then she stops.

Her friend turns too, wearing a look of curiosity.

Dammit. I didn't really think this through, I guess. I would've preferred to do it without an audience, but fuck it. I'm an adult, and I want to get to know this girl.

"Hey, I'm sorry for bothering you." I stop in front of her, thankful I'm not winded. "I didn't really introduce myself back there. I'm Logan. Logan Reid."

She breaks into a small smile. "Hi, Logan."

This close, I realize how tall she is. She's got to be five nine, though I still have a good six inches on her.

2. Bye

"This is kind of bold, and you can totally send me packing, but... can I get your number?"

Chloe squeals, though she quickly snaps her mouth shut and mumbles, "Sorry."

I don't pay her any mind. Yana doesn't either. Her eyes are locked on mine.

She chews on her bottom lip, scanning my face like she's assessing me. For a second, I'm sure she'll shoot me down. But then she nods, and my whole world explodes.

*Fuck yes!*

We exchange numbers, and I wander back into the restaurant. I feel smug as I weave between tables. My steps are light, and my skin is buzzing. The moment I meet Camden's striking blue eyes, though, the sensation dies.

The expression on his face is unreadable.

And no matter how much I want to believe that he's annoyed because of their argument, I know better. I just swooped in and made a move on the girl my best friend very well may have noticed first.

I hope this doesn't bite me in the ass.

ME:

Hi it's Logan, from the other night at the restaurant

I SIT on the bench in the locker room fully dressed, a towel still hanging around my neck, eyes fixed on the screen as I wait for Yana's reply. It took me two days to work up the nerve to text her. Fingers crossed, she'll reply a little more quickly.

Within a minute, my phone dings.

YANA 🏐🔥:

I remember

I chuckle. Maybe it should, but the dry response doesn't surprise me. I looked her up after we met and discovered that some people call her the Snow Queen because of her calm demeanor on the court and during interviews.

ME:

Good. Wasn't sure I made enough of an impression

When she doesn't reply, I click my tongue and type out another message. I need action, and I need to show that I'm interested. My radio silence after I asked for her number showed her the opposite, so it's time to remedy that.

ME:

The team is traveling in 2 days, but I don't want to wait until after to see you

ME:

How about a movie tonight? You choose

YANA 🎾🔥:

Tempting. But my schedule isn't exactly built to work around movies and dates

ME:

Then how about we call it a social skills practice?

YANA 🎾🔥:

Nice try, golden boy

Golden boy? She's already given me a nickname? Warmth radiates through me, and my heart hammers against my ribs. Damn, this little text exchange is fun. Ignoring the commotion in the locker room, I send her a screenshot of the schedule from the movie theater's website.

ME:

What should we see?

YANA 🌕🔥:

The new Marvel

I double-check the time to make sure I can drop off my things at home before our date, then shoot her one last text.

ME:

See you there

I stand and shove my things into my duffel bag. Everything will be wrinkled tomorrow, but I'll worry about that later. My sole focus is to have an amazing date with a stunning girl.

"What's the hurry?" Camden says as I sling the duffel over my shoulder.

He's standing near his locker, a towel wrapped around his hips. His hair is damp, his skin glistening with droplets of water. When I see the ink that covers his arms and neck, I can't help but think about the tattoos I always talked about getting when we were in high school.

He clearly followed through, while I can never find the time.

"I have a date."

He twists his lips. "With that redhead?"

My heart stutters. "With Yana, yes."

With a shake of his head, he shrugs. "Good luck then. See you tomorrow."

I rock back on my heels, a question on the tip of my tongue. Rather than ask, I give him a single nod and head for the door. "Yeah, see you."

If I'm right and he does find her attractive, it's better that I don't know.

WHEN I TEXTED YANA, I thought she'd ignore me or come up with an excuse to say no. Even after she agreed, I figured she'd cancel on me. But she's here, stepping out of a black Escalade as I stand in front of the entrance to the theater. Maybe it's silly, but I brought flowers—a bouquet of purple tulips.

She pulls her coat tight, and when she sees me, she shuffles my way. Her copper-red hair is loose around her shoulders, and for a second my brain goes blank. She was beautiful the other night but also somehow untouchable. Online, she came across as fierce and determined on the court, then elegant and stylish at events.

Now, though? In dark blue jeans, ankle boots, and a black turtleneck under her unbuttoned coat, she's all kinds of perfect.

I fix the collar of the beige shirt that I paired with light brown pants and a dark green bomber as she stops in front of me. "Hey." I hold the flowers up between us. "These are for you."

Smiling, she takes the flowers from me. "Hi, and thank you. They're gorgeous."

"*You* are gorgeous." I grin. "These tulips have nothing on you."

She huffs a laugh. "Do you practice these lines in the mirror, or do they come to you spontaneously? They are way too cheesy, by the way."

"Kind of both." I wink at her. "I already bought tickets. Should we find seats?"

"Sure."

I open the door, and as I follow her inside, I have a hard time taking my eyes off her mouthwatering ass. For the view alone, I'd listen to her mock me all night long.

"Want to share a bucket of popcorn?"

"Sorry, I already had dinner." She gives me a reassuring smile. "And I'm training for my next tournament."

"You're talking to a fellow professional athlete," I remind her. "You don't need to explain yourself to me." Heart thumping in my ears and with a hand on the small of her back, I guide her to the hall. "This way."

During the ads that play before the movie, we chat a little, and once the lights dim and the film starts, she crosses her arms and keeps her gaze on the screen, invested in the plot.

I, on the other hand, have no idea what's happening. All I see is her. The way the corners of her mouth tremble when she's holding back a smile. The way she arches her brow when she's surprised by a scene. But also, the way she shifts in her seat each time our shoulders brush.

By the time the credits roll, I know I'm screwed. This isn't even a free fall. It's a strange, magical type of transportation. My attraction to this girl is already way too consuming.

I've never experienced anything like it.

Outside, the air is crisp. It's a typical California night in December.

"I honestly expected you to bail," I tell her as I walk her to her car, my hands in my pockets.

She smirks, giving me the side-eye. "I considered it."

My chest tightens. "And?"

"And...I'm here, aren't I?" She arches her brow.

My heart stutters, the sensation new and strange. I grin at her anyway. "I'm glad you are."

As we stop by her car, the air between us shifts, and my skin heats. She toys with her car keys, her head tipped down.

I take a tiny step forward, desperate to touch her, my fingertips tingling. "I'll be on the road in two days. Then I have a short break around Christmas before the grind starts up again. When can I see you?"

"I'm not sure." She chews her bottom lip, pressing the tulips to her chest.

My heart stumbles, causing a pang in my chest. Dammit. I was—

"I'll be in Tahoe for Christmas. I rented a cabin for a week." She smiles at me, her gray-green eyes emitting warmth. "I'm training here, but to get myself mentally ready for Australia, I need some time alone, in the woods, surrounded by snow."

I blink, her words sinking in. Honestly, that makes complete sense now that I've done some research on her career.

"You're a brave girl," I murmur.

"I am...most of the time."

Her voice, full of confidence and power, slides right under my skin. God, I'd give anything to get to know her better. To know all her secrets.

I want to know everything about Yana Lipnitskaja.

And I will.

I lean in slowly, zeroing in on her mouth for a moment before making eye contact again. She doesn't move away. Instead, she watches me with interest in her expression. I cup her face and pull her into me. Our mouths meet, and it's like the fucking Fourth of July going off in my head. Her lips are soft and luscious, and I want to devour them. The kiss is slow and soft at first, but when she opens her mouth, I slip my tongue inside, and it quickly becomes heated. Wild, even.

I'm so fucking gone for this girl, it's not even funny.

With my forehead against hers, I confess, "I didn't want to wait to do that till I see you again."

"Good," she murmurs. "But don't get ahead of yourself, Golden Boy."

With that, her lips are on mine. Fuck, I need to figure out how to see her again. Soon.

THREE

# Who Is Golden Boy?

YANA

DRESSED IN PINK PJ'S, WITH A GLASS OF PROSECCO IN HER hand, Chloe sits on my bed. *Gilmore Girls* is playing on the TV, but her attention is on me.

"I can't believe you're really doing it," she mutters for what has to be the third time. "Why can't you stay with me?"

I toss a hoodie into my duffel bag and straighten. "I can't believe you're watching this show again."

She bristles. "This is my comfort show." Tilting to one side, she sets her glass on top of the nightstand. "You're trying to change the subject, and I don't like it." She slides closer to me. "I made all kinds of plans for the Christmas party, and they all included you. I promise it will be a thousand times better than anything you could do in that cabin in the woods."

"I don't even celebrate Christmas on the twenty-fifth." I shake my head. "For me it's just a date on the calendar. I wasn't thinking about parties when I planned this trip."

"Why can't you cancel it?"

I groan and close my eyes. "Physically, I'm ready for the start of the season. My team is happy with the progress I've made, and I am too. I'm really fucking proud of the way I've bounced back." I fix my focus on her. "But mentally? Some things are still too weird, too dark.

I need time alone, away from the noise of the city, to focus on myself. To remind myself why I'm doing all this. So I don't lose sight of my abilities and potential. I'm a good tennis player—"

"One of the best." Chloe snags my hand. "Sorry. I shouldn't push you. And I should've realized you had a damn good reason to go on this solo trip."

"Thank you." I give her hand a squeeze.

My phone buzzes on the flowery comforter, but before I can pick it up, Chloe snatches it and gapes at the screen.

One brow arched, she asks, "Who is Golden Boy?"

*Obyenno*[1].

"No one." I sigh.

A smirk curves her lips. "Pity." She shoves my phone in my face, unlocking the screen in the process, then scrambles off the bed. "Let's see."

Jaw dropping, I stare at her as she darts into the hallway. "Chloe!" I run after her, but before I can catch up, she closes the bathroom door in my face. The moment she screeches, I know she's figured out who Golden Boy is.

"Oh. My. God." She throws the door open, wearing a maniacal grin, no doubt because she's seen the selfies Logan sent me. "Tell me more. Please."

I take my phone from her and return to the bedroom.

She follows me, constantly repeating "tell me more" and "please."

*Love this for me.*

"Yana, I'm begging you. My love life has been as dry as the Sahara Desert. I need some romance to brighten my spirits. Some fresh gossip. Even if it's only a few crumbs." She climbs onto my bed in front of me. "Please, give this little dog a bone!"

Laughter bubbles out of me. She's fucking ridiculous.

"Fine," I huff good-naturedly. "He texted me a couple of days after he asked for my number. Invited me to the movies, and I said

---

1. Awesome (in meaning, but a curse word)

yes." I shrug. "The movie was good. He was nice. I let him kiss me. We've been texting since."

Her jaw drops. "You let Logan Reid kiss you? *The* Logan Reid? The Thunders' left wing? You let him kiss you on *the first date*?"

"It wasn't a big deal." I zip my bag shut a little too aggressively. "We're both athletes. We both have ridiculously busy schedules, so it's better to go ahead and figure out whether we're compatible now rather than waste time dragging it out."

"Wow." Snorting, she slumps. "That's the least romantic thing I've ever heard."

"I was being pragmatic when I agreed to the date. But the kiss was nice. Romantic, even."

"It must have been more than nice. Otherwise, I can't imagine he'd be sending those kinds of selfies to you." Winking, she reaches for her glass. "The one with his abs and the waistband of his pants? Delicious."

"Is sex all you think about?"

She bites her bottom lip, eyes glinting brightly. "Maybe, but only because I haven't been fucked senseless in two months."

"*Pfft*. Must be nice. It's been six for me."

Her jaw drops for the second time tonight.

Annoyance flares in my chest, making my skin itchy.

"For the love of God, text Logan back. Maybe he can dick you down before you leave for your adventure in the woods." She lifts her glass as if she's toasting to the idea. "To your vagina getting some action."

With a roll of my eyes, I pull my phone from my pocket.

GOLDEN BOY:

did you watch the game?

I texted him earlier, congratulating him on his team's win.

ME:

yeah. the team was awesome, especially Roma

GOLDEN BOY:

thanks, but singling out Roman when it was a team effort? rude

GOLDEN BOY:

especially because I'm the one who scored a hat trick

ME:

show-off 🙄

ME:

without the team's amazing defense and your goalie's shutout, your hat trick would've been useless

GOLDEN BOY:

totally get why you and Roman get along so well

GOLDEN BOY:

your honesty is admirable

ME:

sorry 🤪

GOLDEN BOY:

you're lucky I really like you

ME:

or what?

GOLDEN BOY:

or I'd have to make you admit you like me too

I grin at my screen; his confidence is sexy.

"Aww, you're so into him," Chloe murmurs. "You should invite him over. I can leave." She moves to the edge of the bed.

"Sit your ass down," I order her as I set my duffel bag on the floor. "I'm done packing. Let's watch your so-called comfort show together."

Giggling, she obeys, getting comfortable. Just as I climb onto the bed beside her, my phone buzzes again.

GOLDEN BOY:

still going to Tahoe tomorrow? Any fun plans for tonight?

ME:

yeah. my friend's with me

GOLDEN BOY:

have fun then! talk soon

ME:

you too

I toss my phone on the nightstand and focus on the TV. I've seen the entire series before, and it's okay. I'm more of a *Vampire Diaries* kind of girl, or *Supernatural.* Though I also love rewatching old holiday movies in December. That's on my to-do list for my week alone.

"How about sharing with the class?" Chloe nudges me as she sips her drink.

"I'm not exactly good with sharing. Sorry."

She assesses me, a slow smile creeping onto her lips. "Neither am I. I could never share, but I don't think I'd mind *being shared*, if you know what I mean..."

I bang my head against the headboard. "I swear, if—"

"I'm kidding, babe." She laughs. "Only kidding."

I CHECK the GPS and sigh. It's a four-hour drive, but it's early, so once I get to the cabin, I'll have most of the day to relax.

The back seat of my Escalade is filled with two duffel bags and two bags of groceries. The first stretch is nothing but highway. Even this early, traffic slows things down. With an iced latte in my cup holder and a randomly picked playlist—a weird mix of English and Russian songs—at full volume, I sing along, rapping my fingers to the rhythm of the music.

Anything to keep my mind busy.

The longer I drive, the higher the road climbs, and the more the freeway thins out. Once I hit the Sierras, it's like flipping a switch. Pines line the road, tall and endless, their crowns dusted with snow. The crystal blue sky stretches wide, and the view puts a smile on my face. I keep my eyes trained on the road ahead of me as it becomes more winding, slowing me down. I don't mind it at all. The freedom this ride gives me loosens the tight knots in my shoulders that settled in months ago.

When I finally pull up to the cabin, it's like I've fallen down the well in the Brothers Grimm fairy tale "Mother Hulda." Like I've woken up to find myself in a strange and unfamiliar world. The pines are covered in snow, and the ground is a glistening white. I park the car and hurry inside, realizing my ankle-length black jeans, red sneakers, and red hoodie aren't quite weather appropriate.

The cabin looks just like it did in the pictures online. Three bedrooms, a little kitchen, a stone fireplace in the living room. There are no neighbors in sight, but it's still close enough to town that I can make the drive to pick up cheese and milk.

Once I settle in, I call my parents to let them know I made it, then send a few messages to my team and Chloe to check in as well.

The silence around me makes every notification of a reply feel louder. And in the beat after the notification, the quiet is nearly deafening, making me feel lonelier.

While being alone was the whole point of this trip, I can't help but text Logan. Just to see how he is and cut through the quiet.

ME:

made it to the cabin, settled in, turned on Home Alone. what about you?

GOLDEN BOY:

a woman after my own heart. please tell me you also love watching Christmas movies?

ME:

I do. though not only Hollywood ones

GOLDEN BOY:

I'm curious. Want to share titles? Maybe a few you think I'd like?

ME:

nah, they're in Russian

GOLDEN BOY:

Ever heard of these things called subtitles?

ME:

that's the only way I watch movies, genius

GOLDEN BOY:

my point exactly 😉

ME:

I'll think about it and make you a list

GOLDEN BOY:

thanks 😘 what does the cabin look like?

ME:

it's cozy and cute. Definitely has a postcard vibe. though Chloe thinks I'm gonna lose my mind in the silence

GOLDEN BOY:

good thing she's there to keep you company

I blink at the screen. Should I correct him, remind him that I'm here alone? No. He can think whatever he wants.

GOLDEN BOY:

so, Queen, are you texting me because you miss me?

*Queen*? My heart does a stupid little flip, sending my pulse into a sprint.

ME:

just figured I'd let you know, in case I go missing in the woods

GOLDEN BOY:

maybe you should send me your location then

ME:

that's not what I meant

Still, my thumb hovers over the map app longer than it should. It feels reckless. Too personal. No one besides my team, Chloe, and my parents knows where I am. I chew on the inside of my cheek and count to ten. When I still haven't talked myself out of it, I copy my location and drop the pin into the chat.

ME:

there. don't make me regret it

GOLDEN BOY:

never. your secret is safe with me

My skin heats, a pleasant rush of energy swimming in my veins. I put my phone down on the couch and shove it along the cushion, pushing it away. Just to stop myself from making stupid decisions.

Because sending Logan my location was not my smartest move.

By 10 A.M. the next morning, I've laced up my boots so I can take a short walk around the property. To breathe fresh air, to enjoy the view, and simply listen to the quiet. Snow crunches underfoot as I move away from the cabin. The cold wind bites my cheeks, but it only makes me smile wider. This is exactly why I came here. Time away is what I need to restart my brain. To erase all the worries and thoughts about unresolved issues that still plague me.

The scenery reminds me of winter days when I was a child. How my friends and I would go to the school's stadium to sled down the hill, build snowmen, and have snow battles. Once, a classmate hit my best friend Karina in the face with a snowball and ended up giving her a mild concussion.

We promised each other we'd never play with boys again...only to forget about it the next winter.

Those days were happy and so fulfilling. I didn't have the money I have now. I wasn't a world-famous tennis star. I was simply Yana, and life was a thousand times easier.

After lunch, I drive to the closest town. It's beautiful. Snow everywhere, all wooden storefronts and small cafés, and Christmas lights strung across Main Street.

I'm tossing things into a basket when a familiar voice says, "Didn't think you'd actually share your location."

Stomach lurching, I whirl around, coming face-to-face with Logan. All messy blond hair and an easy grin, he stands in front of me in dark blue jeans, a white hoodie, and a dark blue bomber jacket with the Thunders logo on it. His posture is relaxed, as if driving four hours into the mountains on a whim is the most natural thing to do.

Another man wanders up behind him, and when his identity registers, my heart goes into overdrive, hammering against my rib cage. It's that asshole from the restaurant—Camden Hayes, the Thunders' goalie. Yeah, I googled him. I did it because I wanted to know the name of my enemy. Too bad it's hard to despise a man so handsome.

When his eyes fix on mine, my whole body freezes. A heartbeat later, when his piercing blue eyes take me in from head to toe, I heat from the inside out.

His cheeks are red from the cold, and his jet-black hair is messy on top. He's watching me, his arms crossed, dressed in black jeans, a dark blue hoodie, and a leather jacket. His jaw tightens as he takes me in, as if I'm an inconvenience.

Thank God he has no control over his emotions. Like a cold shower, his scowl instantly douses the intrigue that ignited the moment I realized who he was.

"Erm, we had practice this morning," Logan says, his voice snapping me out of my runaway thoughts. "Figured we'd take a drive after. See how you're settling in."

I frown. "That's not—"

"Yeah, yeah, I know." He smiles cheekily. "We stopped here to pick up food and drinks on our way to your cabin, but here you are." He steps closer to me and ducks his head a little. "We have four days off, so I can drive back tonight or tomorrow morning, but I wanted to see you."

Hayes scoffs under his breath, his gaze lingering on me. With a jerk of his head, he looks away, tapping his foot, annoyed.

He isn't the only one. What the hell was Logan thinking driving here without checking with me first? And does he really think I'll let him stay? The worst offense of all is bringing his asshole friend with him. The man who's glaring at me as if he wishes I'd disappear into the floor.

"Logan, I came here alone for a reason," I grit through my teeth. "I only sent you my location in case of an emergency. Not so you'd show up unannounced."

He takes my chin between his thumb and index finger and tilts my face so we're eye to eye. "I'm sorry." He searches my expression, his lips twitching in a small smile. "I didn't mean to upset you. My goal was the opposite, actually. I thought I'd come cheer you up. I won't stay long, I promise. I thought I'd spend time with you today and leave tonight, or in the morning if you'd let me. I'm flying to DC on the twenty-fourth to spend Christmas with my folks, so I can't stay long anyway. Please, Queen, don't be mad."

My knees wobble when that name, Queen, registers. With a sigh, I nod.

"You're incredible." He plants a kiss on my cheek, and as he steps back, he peers around. "Where's your friend?"

*My friend?*

*Chert*[2].

2. Dammit

During our text exchange, he assumed Chloe had come with me, and I never corrected him.

Hayes is watching me intently, wearing an unreadable expression.

Is that why he's here? Because Logan thought there were two of us at the cabin?

"Actually..." I mutter. "I'm here by myself."

FOUR

# You Don't Know Me

YANA

LOGAN'S SMILE DROPS. WITH HIS BROWS PULLED together, he surveys Hayes.

The move alone is enough to confirm my suspicion. Logan invited his friend because he thought Chloe was here too. If I'd corrected him yesterday, we wouldn't have ended up here. How was I to know he'd show up without even bothering to ask if it was okay?

But if I'm honest with myself, I would've eagerly agreed, so why be upset now? He took initiative and made a move. Isn't that what I wanted? Actions, not words?

Regardless, what I didn't want was to come face-to-face with Camden Hayes. He can go screw himself.

"So Chloe's at the cabin, then?" Logan asks, rubbing the back of his neck.

I take a deep breath, and on the exhale, I say, "No. She's back home, working and prepping for her annual Christmas party."

"You've got to be kidding me," Hayes mutters.

He snags Logan's elbow and drags him a few feet away. Heads close, they talk in hushed voices. With the Christmas music playing through the store's speakers, I can't make out a word they say, but their demeanors are easy to read. Logan is calm and collected, while Hayes's expression is sharp, his tone clipped.

I can't help but sympathize with the guy. I hate being blindsided, and he was just as caught off guard as I was. Obviously, Logan had good intentions, and considering our first and only interaction, I can imagine Hayes wouldn't want to touch me with a ten-foot pole.

Though I could be wrong. I don't really know him, except for what I read online.

Honestly, I don't know much about Logan either.

*Kakaya prekrasnaya situacija, s kakoy storony na nee ne posmotri. Pryamo predel mechtanii*[1].

*Bozhe*[2], I loathe just standing here, waiting like this. I shift my weight from one foot to the other, and the move catches Hayes's attention. The intense crystal blue of his irises pins me to the spot and makes my pulse flutter. I reach for the silver pendant on my necklace and fiddle with it, a nervous habit. A wave of heat crashes over me, settling in my lower abdomen and making me press my legs together.

This isn't right.

I open my mouth, eager to break the tension and move this conversation along, but when I do, Camden's gaze drops to my lips. It only remains there for a single inhale, then he's back to looking at his friend.

My shoulders droop when his attention is no longer on me, as if it were the only thing keeping me afloat.

I'm seriously fucked up. The dude probably hates my guts, while just being in his proximity turns me on.

Finally, Logan joins me, his brown eyes warm. He catches a lock of my hair between his fingers and gives me a sincere smile.

"I guess I got a little too excited about the possibility of spending time with you before our schedules get hectic. I forgot that you mentioned you were coming here alone. Or maybe it was wishful thinking." He crooks a smile. "When you mentioned Chloe, I assumed she was with you, and since I was hoping to have you to

---

1. What a wonderful situation, no matter how you look at it. Like the ultimate dream (sarcastic)
2. God

myself for a little while and didn't want your friend to feel like a third wheel, I dragged Camden along with me. He wasn't thrilled, but he is my best friend, so after a little badgering, he agreed. And now here we are."

"Here we are indeed." Despite my initial annoyance, I can't help but grin. I don't know what it is about him, but he makes me feel safe. Just a few minutes in his presence, and the tension in my muscles has nearly vanished. "Can't he drive back home alone?"

"Afraid not." Logan curls his hand around my waist. "We rode together. In my car. If he left, I'd be trapped here, and I'd miss my flight."

"Pity."

"You know I can hear you, right?" Hayes snaps as he stomps back over, tearing my attention away from Logan. Arms folded over his chest, he stands with his lips pressed into a thin line.

"Sorry, man." Logan throws an arm over his friend's shoulder, then peers at me. "I know you came here alone for a reason, and I probably should've asked first. You have every right to tell me to fuck off, but I really hope you'll let us stay. Just one night. We'll leave first thing tomorrow."

Apprehension and curiosity battle in my mind. What do I really lose if I let them stay?

Nothing.

"Okay." I flash Logan a smile. "You're lucky this cabin has three bedrooms."

"Must be my lucky day." He pecks my lips and takes a step back. "What are you shopping for? Maybe we can help."

"How about I finish my shopping, and you pick up whatever you want? Then we can meet in the parking lot."

"Be ready in twenty minutes," Camden barks, already stomping down the aisle.

Logan winks at me. "I better catch up with him. Otherwise, he'll only pick out stuff I don't like. He's a bear when he's in a mood."

"Go get your Grinch, Golden Boy." With that, I turn on my heel.

Before I can go anywhere, he gently grasps my arm and pulls me into him. "Please don't call him that," he says, all his playfulness evaporating. "Literally, you can call him anything else, okay?"

All I can do is nod. I'm not sure how I feel about Camden Hayes, but I'm not mean to people just because. "Of course. Don't worry."

He steals another kiss and then rushes after his friend.

"Yana, *ty idiotka*[3]," I tell myself as I continue my shopping.

TWENTY MINUTES LATER, once my bags are loaded into my Escalade and the guys have loaded theirs into Logan's BMW iX, they follow me to the cabin. The whole way, I listen to another random playlist at full volume, distracting myself from the nervousness that's taken over my body. With the way my stomach roils, I'm not sure I can even eat dinner.

Here and there, I check my rearview mirror. Each time I see Logan's car, my anxiety dissipates a little more. The way he follows at a safe distance adds another point to his rating in my head.

I'll admit, at least to myself, that he's climbing the leaderboard.

And I haven't even slept with him yet. Hell, we haven't even been on the kind of date where we have time to talk. This is so not like me, but maybe that's the appeal of this situation. To live my life without overthinking, without doubting my decisions.

Maybe I can stay in the moment, stay afloat, and let Logan's presence add to the lightness. I feel weightless when he's around. That alone tells me that I'm making the right choice by letting him stay.

As for his best friend? I'm sure it'll be okay. We can just ignore each other.

I park the car and climb out quickly. Evenings always feel darker outside the city, especially during the winter. Snow glimmers under the headlights of Logan's car as he parks behind me. I wait for the

3. you're an idiot

guys, using the time to take in the pine trees crowding the cabin and the road.

Logan climbs out of the car first. A gorgeous smile breaks across his lips. "It's so beautiful." He points up. "The sky is endless out here. And the stars? Damn." Shifting, he takes in the cabin. "Wow, Queen, you're full of surprises. When you said 'cabin,' this is not what I was expecting."

"I dunno," Camden mutters loud enough for me to hear as he unfolds himself from the passenger seat. "A very posh space for a very posh girl. It's exactly what *I* pictured."

Annoyance flares to life in my veins. "You don't know me."

"Agree to disagree." With a chuckle, he opens the back door and retrieves their groceries. "How about we go inside? Early morning practice and four hours in the car have taken their toll on me. I want to eat and sleep. Then I want to get the hell out of here."

Wincing, Logan whispers, "Don't pay him any attention."

Easier said than done, but I'll try. And more than anything, I don't want to ruin my mood, so I let it go.

Logan insists on carrying my grocery bags, and I lead him and his infuriating friend into the cabin. Inside, the warmth of the gas fireplace I had going earlier still lingers in the air.

"Like I mentioned before, there are three bedrooms." I hold an arm out, gesturing down the hall. "I'm in the owner's suite, but the other two are free, and the bedding is clean."

Logan thanks me with that easy smile. Camden just grunts. They drop the groceries in the kitchen, then head back out for their bags. They take their time, probably talking someplace where they won't be overheard. That's fine with me because it gives me time to change into black leggings and a red tee before I return to the kitchen to put our groceries away.

I'm cutting tomatoes when Camden steps into the room. He's still wearing the jeans he arrived in, but instead of a hoodie, he's in a white T-shirt that puts all the tattoos on his neck and arms on display.

Our eyes meet, and my hand falters, the knife hitting the cutting board awkwardly. The effect this guy has on me is destabilizing. One moment, I want to strangle him. The next... No, I better not go there, even in my head.

He is a stranger. Period.

"Do you need help?" he asks, his voice deep and velvety. Its surprising gentleness startles me.

I clear my throat. "No. I'm just slicing tomatoes and cucumbers to have with the chicken cutlets and mashed potatoes I prepped this morning." I set down the knife and survey him. "Do you eat mashed potatoes and chicken cutlets? I didn't even think to ask."

He snorts. "I do. Logan does too, don't worry."

"Good. I'd hate to be a terrible host, even if I didn't plan on having guests."

"You're fine." He takes a few steps closer. "And I'm sorry for being an asshole. I'm tired, but that's no excuse to snap at you. It's not your fault Reid didn't confirm whether your friend was actually here before roping me into this."

"Chloe is single, if you're interested. She's the girl I was with at the restaurant."

He holds my gaze, and that simple act makes me feel like I'm fully naked. "Nah. Your friend is beautiful, but she's not my type."

*Who is your type?* I want to ask.

Instead, I hold out my hand. "I'm Yana. I'm sure you know that by now, but we started off on the wrong foot and never introduced ourselves."

The smirk that pulls at his lips is pure sin. And those dimples? Fuck.

"I'm Camden." He wraps his big, calloused hand around mine, immediately engulfing me in his warmth. "It's very nice to meet you."

Neither of us takes a step back. Neither of us lets go. Eyes locked, we stand in the quiet of the kitchen, assessing each other.

"Sorry it took me so long." Logan's voice reaches the kitchen before he does.

Camden lets go of my hand and backs up. The step he takes is so big, it leaves him standing at the kitchen entrance.

Logan steps inside and glances between us. "What are you two up to?"

"Just finally introducing ourselves," I say, ignoring how fast my heart beats inside my chest. "And I'm cutting vegetables to go with the chicken cutlets I made for dinner." I pick up the knife again. "Your best friend told me you'd like them."

Grinning, Logan drapes his big arm over Camden's shoulder. "And he'd be right."

Yin and yang indeed. They remind me of that boy band that was popular years ago in the Russian-speaking world—one was blond, the other had nearly black hair. How did that connection not hit me sooner?

"Would you guys set the table?" I ask as I turn back to the cutting board.

When they've collected supplies and moved to the dining room, I close my eyes and take a few deep breaths to steady myself.

I didn't expect Camden to apologize for his behavior. Not after the way he acted in the restaurant and at the store. But I can't say I'm not happy he did.

Who knows, maybe we can spend this one evening together without being at each other's throats.

FIVE

# My Favorite Kind of Dessert

LOGAN

AT DINNER, OUR CONVERSATION REMAINS SURFACE-LEVEL. Mostly, we talk about the food and our favorite dishes. The three of us sit at the wooden table in the corner of the cabin. Its matching chairs and the coordinating bookshelves create a rustic vibe, though the place is anything but. The dining area is open to the living room, making it one big space, and the place is equipped with everything a guest could need.

Camden watches Yana's every move, and he hangs on to her every word. He tries to hide it, but I know him well enough to see the subtleties. The way he swallows thickly each time she smiles, the way his jaw tightens when I lean into her. I've never asked for confirmation, but I'm pretty sure he noticed her first. It'd be a lie if I said it didn't eat at me. Every day—hell, every hour—my attraction to her grows. Knowing that my best friend, the one guy who knows every part of me, is attracted to her too makes me fucking jealous.

But there's another sensation there too, something hotter. A jolt of excitement hits me every time I consider that he might want her as badly as I do. I shouldn't like it. I should want to shut it down, claim her, make it clear she's mine. Yet when his eyes track her, my pulse spikes in a way I can't explain.

The stone fireplace is tall and wide. It's the room's focal point, with a big sectional and a coffee table in front of it. One of the first things I noticed when I stepped into the cabin was the absence of a Christmas tree. There's not a single sign of the approaching holiday. Does that mean she isn't celebrating it?

I decide to go for it.

"You don't like Christmas?" I ask.

The warm lighting emphasizes her freckles as she shifts and tucks her hair behind her ear. "Why would you think that?"

Camden beats me to it, saying, "There's no Christmas tree. No lights. Literally nothing."

"I do like Christmas." She sighs. "But I don't celebrate it on the 25th. The orthodox church I belong to celebrates it on January 7th, so we tend to celebrate and exchange gifts on January 1st." She sets her glass on the table. "For my family, Christmas is more like a secular holiday. An opportunity for us to get together more than anything." She glances at Camden, then at me. "Though after I'd been in the US for a couple of years, I got more into the Christmas spirit. I normally put up a Christmas tree in my apartment, but it felt unnecessary this year since I won't be home. And I'm only here for a week, so decorating the cabin seems silly."

The more she talks, the more I realize how much I like her voice. She has an accent, but her words are soft. Like she's good at meeting the tone of the person speaking to her, mimicking their habits and pronunciations.

"Roman mentioned that, but I didn't pay much attention at the time," Camden drawls. "He said his family celebrates Christmas twice."

Smiling, Yana nods. "Yup. I've been to parties at their house on January 7th and also on the 25th." She takes a sip of her apple juice. "What about you two? Do you celebrate Christmas?"

Camden's smile slips, and he lowers his focus to his plate. Fuck. I should've mentioned this when I asked her not to call him the Grinch. All because his late granny used to call him that whenever he wasn't in the mood close to Christmas.

"I love Christmas," I chime in, cutting through the awkwardness that's swept over us. "I usually spend the holiday with my parents and my little sister, Lucy. This year, she might be more excited for my visit than Santa's."

A bolt of laughter springs out of Yana's mouth. "What did you promise your little sister that has her so excited?" She tilts her head to the side. "And how little are we talking?"

"A new iPad with an Apple pencil. And she's eight."

Yana's mouth falls open, and her eyes go wide. "Your sister is..." She peers up at the ceiling, a crease between her brows. "She's seventeen years younger than you?"

"Yup." I can't help but smirk. This woman knows how old I am? Interesting. "Did you google me?"

She snorts. "I did, and I'm a hundred percent sure you did the same for me."

I wince playfully. "Guilty."

The air between us shifts, becoming more charged. Our glances linger, the tone of our voices heavier. The flirting more pronounced. It all screams mutual attraction, and I honestly can't wait to be alone with Yana. The way I want her is mind-blowing.

I've never craved a woman more than I crave this one.

"What about you, Camden?" she asks, ripping me out of my thoughts.

Fuck.

*Note to self: No daydreaming about a girl when you should be checking in with your best friend and the pain he carries surrounding the most traumatic experiences of his life.*

Tongue pressed to the inside of his cheek, he keeps his focus trained on the wall ahead of him.

I straighten, ready to intercept, but before I can, he opens his mouth and says, "I've always loved Christmas and New Year's. But two years ago, my granny died right before Christmas. My parents died in a car crash when I was nine, and after that, she raised me. Now I don't have anyone to celebrate it with, so this time of year is hard."

A heavy silence settles between us.

Camden has an unreadable expression on his face, while Yana's eyes fill with tears. I sit back, racking my brain for a topic that will lighten up the mood.

"Oh my God," Yana mutters. "I'm so sorry."

She reaches over, probably intending to grab his hand on the table, but he clocks the movement, and before she has a chance to touch him, he retracts his hand and picks up his glass.

"Sorry for ruining the mood." He downs his whiskey and stands. "Let's find a movie to watch."

"Yeah, sure," she mumbles, meeting my gaze.

"Sorry," I mouth.

With a shake of her head, she stands and starts collecting dishes. I help her clear the table and rinse the plates so she can load them into the dishwasher. When we return to the living room, Camden is sitting on the edge of the couch, his elbows on his knees, his expression still drawn.

"Logan mentioned you were watching *Home Alone* last night," he says quietly, avoiding looking at either of us. "I thought maybe we could watch *Home Alone 2*?"

"Sounds good." I settle on the other side of the couch.

Yana joins me, letting me drape my arm around her shoulder and tuck her into my chest. Her hair smells like cinnamon and apple, a scent I've always associated with Christmas. When she laughs, the sound reverberates through my body. Even our breaths are in sync now, calm and comfortable.

Twenty minutes in, Camden pushes off the couch. His eyes shoot straight to us and linger, his jaw rigid. "I'm tired. Gonna turn in." His voice sounds flat. "Night."

I nod.

"Night," Yana responds.

With that, he strides away, leaving the two of us alone. Within minutes, it's clear that neither of us is interested in watching the movie any longer.

Yana tilts her face up to me, her gray-green eyes bright in the glow of the TV screen, and I don't think twice. I tighten my hold and kiss her. It's slow and gentle at first, and when she sighs into my mouth, I slip my tongue past her lips and deepen the connection, running my hands down her sides, feeling her up, relishing her curves.

She breaks the kiss suddenly, her breath ragged, and stands. With her hand held out to me, she whispers, "Come with me."

I thread my fingers through hers as she leads me to her bedroom, my heart pounding.

We don't turn on the light, so the room is dim, the moon outside the only source of light.

She takes a deep breath, then licks her lips. "This may not be the best way to set the mood, but this is how I am." Shoulders pulled back, she clears her throat. "We're both athletes. Our lives are ridiculously busy. Travel, training, tournaments, press events." She steps into me and places her hand on my chest. "If there's something between us, I'd rather find out now than drag this out and play games. Being intimate with my partner is important to me, so I want to know now if we can make it work. If we have what it takes to have mind-blowing sex."

Her honesty, her confident tone, and the way she tells me what she wants while holding her head high? Ten out of fucking ten.

Gripping her waist, I hold her gaze. "I'm with you. No waiting. No bullshit." I angle closer, my mouth at her ear. "And trust me, Queen, we have what it takes to have mind-blowing sex."

"Big words." Her hot breath fans over my face.

"From a big guy." I cover her mouth with mine, teasing her at first, giving her gentle pecks here and there. But as I explore her body with my hands, the kiss grows more intense, our lips glued to each other, our tongues tangled. I kiss her with everything I have, with all the burning passion that ignited in me the moment I saw her at the store a few hours ago.

"Fuck, I love kissing you," I murmur against her neck.

Moaning, she throws her head back. "It feels so good..."

With a deep sense of satisfaction, I suck the sensitive skin there into my mouth. She grips my shoulders, digging her fingers into my flesh through my tee. It only spurs me on, causing me to leave a trail of love bites down her neck.

"You're lucky I'm into this stuff." She giggles as she pulls me closer to the bed. "Trying to mark your territory, Golden Boy?"

I chuckle. "I'm not trying to do anything." I push her slightly, easing her onto the sheets. "After tonight, you'll know you're mine." Bending, I gently grip her chin and lift her face. "Take your T-shirt off. Red looks good on you, but I'd prefer you without it."

With a nod, she obeys, tossing the tee to the floor.

And her perfect body captivates me. It's carved from years of discipline and hard work. She's all lean muscle, straight shoulders, and toned arms. Her tits are round, her nipples perky, begging me to curl my tongue around them. And her narrow waist and killer abs? This woman is a work of art, and I'll be damned if I'm not going to spend the night worshiping every inch of her.

"Don't go quiet on me," she says softly. "And take off your shirt. I want to see you too."

Without hesitation, I rip off my T-shirt, flexing my muscles as I do. Giving her a show. Then, with my eyes locked on hers, I kneel in front of her and put my hands on her legs.

She plants her hands on the mattress and lifts her hips, allowing me to slide off her leggings and expose the lacy red panties beneath. *Fuck*. Heart hammering, I grab her hips and pull her toward me, draping her legs over my shoulders.

"Now lie back and let me enjoy my dessert." I kiss her inner thigh, then suck her skin into my mouth, leaving another mark.

Slowly, I tease her, driving her out of her mind. Eventually, I push her panties aside, revealing her glistening pussy.

*Goddammit*. I lean in eagerly and circle her clit with my tongue.

A moan slips out of her mouth, filling my chest with pride.

If she continues to respond to me like that, then I'm in for a real treat.

I suck and lick, palming her perfect breasts, rolling her nipples, picking up my pace. Before she goes over the edge, I slow down. Her moans and whimpers get louder as I build her up again and again.

"More," she begs. "More, please..." She rolls her hips, rubbing her juices all over my face.

I double my efforts, sucking her clit into my mouth, then grazing my teeth over it.

Her breath goes ragged, and I know she's chasing her orgasm. So I push one finger inside her and ravish her clit. When she responds with a long, low moan, I add a second finger, then a third.

"You taste so delicious, babe," I murmur against her heat. "Like my favorite kind of dessert."

I fuck her with my fingers, crooking them to hit her sweet spot while I lap her clit with my tongue, speeding up my movements with each passing second. My digits drip with a mixture of my saliva and her juices.

"Oh, *bozhe*[1]..." She cries out, gripping the sheets, when I suck hard on that little bundle of nerves.

Her pussy spasms, then her whole body trembles as her orgasm washes over her. I don't stop my movements as she rides out her release.

Only when her pussy is no longer contracting around me do I stand and lower myself onto the bed beside her. I prop myself up on one elbow and take in her flushed cheeks and the way her chest heaves.

With a lazy smile, she opens her eyes. "What are you, a pussy-eating champ?"

Laughter rumbles out of me as I shake my head. "Just wanted to give you the queen treatment, that's all." I cover her lips with mine, kissing her slow and gentle as I bury my hand in her hair.

Without pulling away, she unbuttons my jeans and lowers the zipper. I'm hit with a wave of relief when the fabric straining against my rock-hard cock gives, making me double my efforts.

"I need you out of your jeans." She rears back. "Take them off."

"Yes, ma'am." I wiggle out of them, then shuck off my briefs. "Though you need to get rid of your panties too. They'll be in the way."

With a sinful smile, she shimmies out of them. Then she sits up

---

1. God

and assesses me, catching her bottom lip between her teeth as she zeroes in on my dick.

I wrap my hand around my shaft and give it a few pumps, teasing us both.

"Sit up. Against the headboard," she orders.

I do as I'm told. Once I'm settled, she climbs onto my lap, straddling me, and grasps my dick.

"I have an implant," she says, her focus on my face. "Had it put in a couple of months ago."

The meaning of her words dawns on me as she hoists herself up. Before she can impale herself on me, I grasp her waist, stalling her for a moment.

"You sure?" I swallow thickly. "I was tested at the beginning of the season, and they were all negative, but—"

"Mine too," she whispers, guiding my dick to her pussy. "And I'm sure."

I smirk, and with a deliberate slowness, I pull her down onto my cock. "Fuck."

She's wet, warm, and tight. So goddamn perfect. She feels like fucking heaven.

She slides up and down my shaft, making my eyes roll back in my head. With each curve of her hips, she takes me deeper and deeper. When she's fully seated, I swear I see fucking constellations in my mind, and they all have one name—Yana.

Head bent, I swirl my tongue over one pert nipple, the move causing her to throw her head back and moan. Her reaction spurs me on, and I do it again, and again, and again. Each time, she only moans louder. Movements fast and choppy, she grasps the headboard, using it for leverage.

"Fuck, babe," I pant. "If you keep moving your hips like that, I'm not gonna last long."

Fire forms in my lower abdomen. It's slow and small at first, but with each dip of her hips, it burns brighter, wilder. With my hands splayed over her hips, I help her move faster. She fucks me hard and rough, the rhythmic sound of the headboard hitting the wall the soundtrack to our desire.

It takes me too long to realize just how loud we're being.

Camden.

Fuck.

I cup the back of her head and make her look at me.

"We need to keep quiet. If we don't, Camden will know exactly what we're doing in here."

Her mouth falls open, her eyelids heavy. Then she breaks into a slow smile. "I think he already knows. I'm not particularly quiet."

A zing of excitement rushes through my veins like a bolt of lightning in the sky. For some fucked-up reason, the idea of Camden knowing what we're doing turns me on even more. It's not because I feel smug as fuck for getting the girl. But the idea of him listening to us sends a hot energy to my cock.

I wonder how it would feel to have him watch us...*fuck*. Just the imagery alone brings me closer to the edge.

I grip Yana's hips tighter, dragging her over me, giving her everything I've got, and she meets me thrust for thrust. With her lips on mine, she rides me fast and rough, stealing the air from my lungs.

"Fuck," I mumble as she clenches around me.

Her body convulses slightly as she orgasms for the second time, and that triggers my own release, my reaction far more violent than hers. I hide my face in the hollow of her neck, panting and breathing heavily as I come down from the high. My forehead is pressed to her sweaty skin, and her scent fuses with mine, making my head spin.

That was the best sex of my life. Hands fucking down.

"Think you'd be up for another round soon?" she whispers.

With a snort, I shift so I can look her in the eye. "A woman after my own heart indeed."

## SIX

# We're Stuck Here

YANA

A SHARP KNOCK ON THE DOOR STARTLES ME OUT OF A DEEP sleep. I snap my eyes open, and when I realize I can't move, horror seizes my lungs.

Before I can go into fight-or-flight mode, it dawns on me that Logan's wrapped around me from behind, and he's holding me tight to his chest. I close my eyes and melt into him, but another knock sounds, making my muscles tense. This time, the sound is followed by Camden's voice.

"Reid, dammit, answer the door. I know you're in there."

I wiggle out of Logan's arms and nearly tumble out of bed. I scurry around, collecting my tee and leggings from the floor. I get dressed, and then, tentatively, I crack open the door and poke my head out. Instantly, I find myself ensnared by a pair of crystal blue eyes.

Camden is wearing a black tee, black pants, and a menacing scowl. Clearly, he's not a morning person.

"Where is Reid?" he demands.

"Asleep."

He tsks. "Then wake him up."

My stomach sinks. "Is something wrong?"

"Wake him up," he grits through his teeth. "Reid!" he calls, peering over me. "Get your fucking ass out of bed."

Goodness, is he always this cranky in the morning?

I frown. "What's wrong with you?"

"Nothing is wrong. My life is *perfect*," he snaps. "Reid!"

"For fuck's sake," Logan grumbles behind me.

I glance back, and when I catch him climbing out of bed completely naked, a wave of heat crashes over my body, making me clench my legs together. This man's body is a fucking masterpiece: broad shoulders, muscular arms and thighs, and his ass? I gripped it more than once last night, relishing his tight, toned glutes. But the way it looks in broad daylight? I've never seen anything more beautiful.

He pulls on his sweatpants and strolls over, his lazy smile making my knees weak. I'm so smitten with him it's ridiculous.

Before he fixes his attention on his friend, he stops beside me and kisses my temple. "Good morning."

"Morning," I murmur into his neck.

"What's the emergency?" Logan asks as he tucks me into his side.

Camden squares his shoulders, filling the doorframe with his presence. "Roads are closed. A storm came in overnight. So we're stuck here. From what I can tell, the roads won't be cleared until the 26th."

My stomach drops, and I blink rapidly, like maybe that will help me make sense of his words.

There's no way, right?

Logan clears his throat, his body tensing beside me. "What do you mean?"

"Just what I said." Camden shrugs, though the movement belies the tension radiating off him. "We're fucking stuck here, Reid. Because of you."

"Fuck." Logan steps away and rubs a hand down his face. "Lucy is gonna be so upset."

"No shit, man. Though your little sister is the least of your problems because I'm pissed, and I'm the one you're stuck here with." Camden quickly assesses me, his jaw ticking. Then he focuses on Logan. "I knew better than to let you talk me into this. Coming here was a mistake."

My chest pangs, the sensation uncomfortable. His words hurt, and I don't know why. Who cares if he's upset?

It shouldn't matter...but it does. It fucking does.

"I need to call my parents." Logan steps out of the room, forcing Camden to move back. "They're gonna kill me."

"Tell them to get in line because I'm gonna kill you first." He stomps after Logan as he makes his way to the room next door.

Shaking my head, I close the door and give myself some time to recenter. A quick shower will wake me up and maybe help me sort out my thoughts. Because this strange feeling in my gut worries me. Sure, I'm annoyed about being stuck here with them, since my goal was time alone to rest and reset. Yet that's not what concerns me.

The two of them and me, trapped here, with nowhere to go and not much to do. For at least two days, if what Camden said is correct.

My body heats, and the tepid water raining down on me does nothing to cool me off.

This is not good, not good at all.

AFTER MY SHOWER, I twist my hair into a messy bun on top of my head and pull on leggings and a loose T-shirt. The neckline instantly slides down my shoulder, exposing the fact that I'm not wearing a bra, but I couldn't care less. I'm here to relax and feel at ease. Logan hasn't come back to the room, but his voice drifts to me through his closed bedroom door once I step into the hallway, hinting that he's still on the phone with his parents.

I wander into the kitchen, set on cooking breakfast, but I stop short at the threshold. Camden's already standing at the stove, his back looking impossibly broad as he flips the bacon in the hissing pan.

"You didn't have to do that," I say, stepping closer. "I was going to make—"

"Too late," he mutters without looking up.

Irritation bubbles to life inside me. "Excuse me?"

He breaks an egg with a quick, practiced movement, the white and yolk quickly settling into the preheated pan. "I figured you'd be too tired. In fact, I thought you'd gone back to bed, so I decided I'd save you the trouble." He breaks another egg into the pan. "Plus, I didn't want to starve to death."

I blink. His explanation makes no sense. "What are you talking about?"

He finally looks at me, lips twisted. "You had a long night, right?"

Warmth that has nothing to do with the heat of the stove creeps into my cheeks.

*Chyert by ego pobral*[1].

I grit my teeth, willing my hands not to tremble. "The walls aren't *that* thin."

"Thin enough." He holds my gaze. The look he gives me is steady, challenging, pinning me to the spot and making me feel exposed. It's like he wants me to know he heard everything. "And you aren't particularly quiet."

The words hang in the air, heavier than they should be, sending my pulse skyrocketing. The heat in my cheeks has consumed me completely. I don't know what I want to do more—argue with him that my sex life is not for his entertainment, or walk away so I can chide myself in private.

Before I can do or say anything, Logan strolls in. He's in a white T-shirt and gray sweatpants, his blond hair dusted with snow and his cheeks red. "Stepped outside to assess the situation after my phone call. It's fucking freezing." Shivering, he steps into me and slips his hand around my waist. "And there's snow everywhere. Our cars are buried under it. It'll be good to clear the snow off them later today."

"What did your parents say?" I ask, trying to ignore Camden's presence.

"They're disappointed. Lucy too." He flashes me a cute smile. "Though the moment I promised to make it up to her with another gift, I was forgiven." He flicks his attention to Camden. "Mom and

1. Damn him.

Dad said hi, and they asked me to remind you about their invitation. They'd love it if you joined us."

"Thanks." He nods, his eyes sliding to where Logan's hand rests at my waist. His jaw twitches, but he says nothing, just returns his focus to the stove. "Breakfast's ready. Could you two set the table?"

"Sure." I untangle myself from Logan and pull plates from the cabinet, ignoring their murmurs behind my back.

This whole situation is just a bump in the road. A little hiccup. I've been under way more pressure during tournaments. This is nothing in comparison.

*Nadeyus' ya sama nachnu v eto verit*[2].

ONCE THE KITCHEN is clean and our stomachs are full, Logan and I snuggle on the couch in the living room, and Camden sits on the floor by the fireplace. It's only one o'clock, and the day seems endless. If I were alone, I would be watching movies, reading, and dancing around in my pj's. Now, I'm trying to think of a way to keep all of us entertained.

"Any plans for today?" I ask no one in particular.

Camden snarls. "Yeah. My plans included going to the rink, then the gym. Instead, I'm rotting here on the floor until bedtime." He narrows his eyes at me, then at Logan. "I'd be grateful if one of you could find some earplugs for me. I have no interest in listening to the two of you go at it again."

"Stop being so bitter," Logan grouses, tightening his hold on me. "You almost sound condescending."

"Really? Almost? Too bad. Because that's what I was going for." He shrugs.

I roll my eyes and take a deep breath. He's going to make this place feel like hell, isn't he?

2. I hope I'll start believing it myself.

"How about we watch a movie?" Logan asks. "That worked out pretty well last night."

"Speak for yourself," Camden mutters. Then he inhales loudly. "Fine. Whatever." His gaze lands on me, his brow arched. "What's on your list? Just the *Home Alone* movies?"

"No, but we should probably finish *Home Alone 2*. Then we can watch *Home Alone 3*." I give him a feral smile. "After that, we can make dinner."

"Please tell me there are other movie options for after dinner." He continues studying me, his intensity setting my skin on fire.

"Absolutely. I'll even let you pick." I hold his gaze, refusing to back down.

Logan plants a kiss on my temple. "Sounds good."

Camden hauls himself up, keeping his gaze averted. "I better get myself a beer. I'm gonna need it to survive all these cheesy movies."

"Bring some for us too," Logan calls as his friend stomps toward the kitchen.

"Not for me," I chime in. "I don't drink this early."

Camden stops in his tracks and smirks at us. "Get your own," he says to Logan. "You're a big boy."

With a sigh, Logan releases me and stands. "And he's being a big, fat baby," he mumbles as he follows Camden.

*Home Alone 2* is a hit. Within minutes, the atmosphere in the room relaxes. We talk and joke, mostly about the movie and its actors. It's comfortable, even. I drink juice, and the boys drink beer.

Once the movie is over, I go to the kitchen for snacks. A second later, Logan joins me.

"Finally." He pads across the room, eyes fixed on me. "A moment alone."

He backs me against the kitchen counter, his hands on my hips, his breath hot on my skin as he captures my lips with his. The kiss is slow and sweet, the alcohol on his tongue making me a little dizzy.

Until a sudden thud startles us.

Camden stands beside the fridge, another beer bottle in his hand. "Sorry," he grumbles as he strides out of the room.

"Is he always like that?" I whisper. "Or is it because of me?"

Logan slides a hand through his hair. "Not exactly..." He winces. "And yeah, it might be because of you."

My stomach sinks, but I shrug off the sensation. "He hasn't been a fan since we first met, so I shouldn't be surprised."

"I don't think..." He shakes his head. "Don't let him get to you. It'll be fine."

"If you say so." I force a smile. "He's your best friend."

With one more peck to my lips, Logan snags another beer from the fridge and heads out of the room.

When I'm alone, I let my shoulders droop. Why does Camden have to make everything so difficult? Ugh. Bedtime cannot come fast enough.

In the living room, I put on *Home Alone 3* and cuddle with Logan. Every time he laughs, the sound reverberates through my body, bringing a smile to my face and a fuzzy feeling to my stomach. I'm calmer, happier, than I've been in months. Not even Camden's constant scoffs and complaints about how this movie pales in comparison to the first two can ruin my mood.

When the credits roll, Camden, who's refused to sit on the couch all day, shifts, glancing up at me from the floor. "What's next? Since you're the one set on this movie marathon."

"Should we make dinner before we start another movie?" I ask, ignoring his question.

"I'm in." Logan stands.

Camden holds my gaze. "Me too. But first, I'd like to know what we're going to watch next."

"I have the perfect movie, and I bet you've never seen it." I grin, leaning back against the cushions. "How about *Ivan Vasilievich Changes His Profession*?"

Logan tips back the last of his beer. "Wait—what?"

Camden just stares at me, his eyebrows pulled together.

I pluck my phone from the coffee table and google the name of the movie. "Oh, that's the literal translation. According to this"—I hold up my phone—"in English it's called *Ivan Vasilievich: Back to the*

*Future*."

Logan laughs. "So it's a rip-off of an American movie, then?"

"No." I huff, annoyed and maybe a bit defensive. "This one came first. It's based on a play by Bulgakov, actually. And it's hilarious."

"Bulgakov?" Camden says in a low voice.

I blink at him, sitting straighter. "Yeah. Do you know about Bulgakov?"

"Of course." He lifts his bottle and takes a sip. "He's the author of *The Master and Margarita*."

I don't know what surprises me more, his casual tone, or the fact that he knows who Bulgakov is at all.

Either way, his response and the heat in his eyes warm my skin and make my heart thud heavily.

"You read Bulgakov?" I ask.

He shrugs, but when he speaks, his voice cracks. "My grandma loved him. Made me read his stuff with her. She basically forced me into a two-person book club, where we read and then discussed each book."

The room goes quiet, the only sound coming from the storm that's assaulting the cabin walls and windows.

Logan shifts beside me, but I can't take my eyes off Camden.

The way he explained his knowledge—not to show off, but as if reminiscing about a part of his past he clearly loved and misses—hits me firmly in the solar plexus. His tone is tainted with grief and a sadness that feels heavier than the weight of even my biggest problems. Seeing him so vulnerable, with his emotions written all over his face, softens my heart.

Camden Hayes is not the man I thought he was. There's a surprising tenderness under all his bite and sharpness.

If he'd shown me that side of him the night we met, things between us might be very different.

My chest tightens at the thought, my pulse quickening. The sensation that's creeping in is wrong in so many ways, especially while Logan's arm is draped over my shoulders. But there's no denying it's there.

## SEVEN

# Not Until Her

### CAMDEN

"I'M CURIOUS," LOGAN ASKS, DICING A TOMATO. "IF WE hadn't shown up, what would you be doing right now?"

I force myself not to look at Yana while waiting for her answer, but the effort is in vain. She's beside me, stirring chicken and veggies in a pan on the stove as I drain the pasta. If I shifted an inch or two, my shoulder would brush hers. It's tempting, but I stay put. At least this I can control, unlike my wandering eyes.

Her hair is up in a messy bun, with a few wild locks framing her face. Her leggings hug her toned legs so perfectly that every time I look at her ass, my own sweatpants get tight. I don't think I've ever wanted a woman more than I want this one.

It's wrong. She and my best friend clearly have a connection, but every moment I spend with her only makes me crave her more. And I can't even blame it on the thrill of the forbidden, since I've been attracted to her from the very first moment my eyes landed on her at the restaurant.

*She's with Logan, dude. Forget it.*

Yana laughs, peering at Logan over her shoulder. "Pretty much what we're doing now. My plan was to relax and do the things that bring me joy. That includes watching holiday movies, listening to my favorite music, dancing, and maybe a little doomscrolling."

"Would you have chosen the same movies?" I ask.

Brows raised, she inspects me. I've spent most of the day either ignoring her or snapping at her and Logan, so it's no surprise that she looks like I stunned her speechless.

"Um...yeah," she eventually forces out. "Though I probably would've watched more Russian movies." She shrugs. "I didn't discover *Elf* until a few years ago, and I can't say that I love *love* it, you know? It's a great movie and very Christmasy, but I don't rewatch it every year like just about everyone I know. I wasn't going to watch it this year...but here we are."

"If you don't want to watch it, then why did you suggest it?" I set the pasta on the counter and add the sauce she threw together.

"Because you mentioned it. Several times."

For a moment, we're silent. Then Logan barks out a laugh. Yana joins in, and despite my best efforts, I do too. Damn, she got me. I kept pushing after she suggested an old soviet movie and a couple others I'd never heard of.

"If you don't want to watch it, we really don't have to. We should watch something you like," I say, stirring the pasta into the sauce. "It doesn't matter whether I watch *Elf* for the hundredth time or not."

I hold her gaze, and when she watches me just as intently, my body sizzles with heat. It's probably the alcohol and our proximity. There's no way I'm really thirsting after my friend's girl in a way that makes me imagine the most reckless kind of shit.

Behind us, Logan clears his throat, breaking the moment. She instantly turns to face him, putting her back to me.

"I'm with Cam. We showed up unannounced and threw your schedule off, so please, don't change anything because of us."

"Thank you." She turns off the stove, ducking her head for a moment. "Chicken is ready."

"I'm done with the salad," Logan states, lifting the bowl from the counter. "How about the pasta?"

I hum. "Pasta is ready too."

Yana looks between us, a mischievous smile tipping up her lips.

"The last person to say 'Aye, Captain' sets the table. One, two, three—"

"Aye, Captain." She and Logan shout in unison.

I arch a brow, doing my best not to roll my eyes. "You're like kids."

Logan says, "Look who's talking," but I ignore him.

I don't mind setting the table, actually. It'll give me a minute to myself, and I fucking need it.

"Go sit. I'll bring out plates and silverware in a minute." I nod toward the dining table.

Without a word, they shuffle out of the kitchen. As I gather what I need, I check the time. It's already seven. Thank fuck. Only a couple more hours before I can escape this hell and hole up in the bedroom.

I'm already third-wheeling, and the later it gets, the more obvious it becomes.

THIS OLD MOVIE turns out to be pretty funny. We laugh at the absurdity of some of the scenes, and occasionally Logan asks Yana to skip back a few seconds because he didn't catch the subtitles.

Overall, the evening has gone much better than I expected. I don't understand why Yana considers this a Christmas movie, but I decide not to question her.

I'd probably put my foot in my mouth again, and I don't need to ramp up the tension in here. It's hard enough having to sit near them while they're glued to each other.

After dinner, the three of us settle in with our own bottles of beer. Yana's cheeks are now pink, her eyes glistening in the shimmering light of the TV in the otherwise dark room.

Logan's got her tucked against him on the couch, his arm slung over her like it's the most natural thing in the world. She fits in his arms perfectly, laughing softly when the subtitles are incorrect, tilting her head toward him when he asks about the movie.

I shouldn't care.

I tell myself that over and over. But I do. I'm acutely aware of their every move. Every fucking time she wiggles against him, it feels like a blade is sliding under my ribs. This jealousy is unhealthy, especially because I have no right to feel it.

Sure, I saw her first, but Logan was the one who made a move. He asked her on a date; he kissed her first. All I did was piss her off by opening my fucking mouth and acting like an asshole.

I am no match for Logan. He's always been the golden one, the guy people can't help but be drawn to, even when we were kids. It's never bothered me before now. I've never been envious of how easy it is for him to get a girl, to make new friends. I'm the prickly one. The asshole. The bad boy to his good guy persona.

My granny used to joke that Logan and I were like yin and yang, balancing each other, complementing one another, bringing out the best in each other. It felt good, thinking I could have that kind of impact on him. It still does, most days. But what's happening to me as I watch him hold Yana makes me want to tear the whole scene apart.

I've never wanted anything that belonged to him. Not until her.

When the movie ends, I turn, ready to toss the remote to Yana so she can pick out another one. Instead, I freeze, my lungs seizing up. Because the two of them are locked in a passionate kiss.

Fuck. This is the last thing I need.

I scramble to my feet and stride for the kitchen without looking back. "I need a beer."

Counting to fifty in my head, I stand with my back pressed to the fridge.

Their voices drift in from the living room, but I try my best to ignore them. One more hour, and I'll lock myself away in my room. But I could use a few more drinks to help me sleep. Especially if they start fucking again.

"Get yourself together," I hiss.

I snatch a bottle from the fridge, twist the cap, and head back out. Just as I hit the threshold, Yana's there, laughing under her breath and looking over her shoulder. Her body collides with mine, and she stumbles, a hitching breath leaving her parted lips. I snake my arm around her waist, pressing her against my chest to steady her.

She meets my gaze, eyes wide and pupils blown out.

My palm, splayed over her lower back, burns. She licks her lips, and the movement garners my attention, tempting me to study her inviting mouth. I want her. God, I want her so bad, it takes everything in me not to kiss her.

I need to leave.

I drop my hand from her waist and take a step back. "Sorry." With a tight smile, I skirt around her. Dammit. It's gonna take way more than a few more drinks to erase the feeling of her against me.

"Everything all right?" Logan asks as I slump onto the floor.

"Yeah." I take a sip of my drink, forcing myself to look at him. "What are we watching?"

He chuckles, unaware of the war raging inside my head. "*A Christmas Carol.*"

"Okay."

"Have you seen it before?" Yana returns from the kitchen, the sound of her voice capturing my attention like a siren's song. She hands a beer to Logan, then slips in beside him again, holding her own beer bottle.

"I don't remember. Maybe." I stare at the TV, determined not to look away until the clock strikes ten and I can bow out for the night.

But no matter how hard I try, I can't stop thinking about how she felt against me. How my skin ignited when I touched her. So, instead of distracting myself with the movie, I end up sneaking glances at her and Logan.

She's sitting between Logan's legs now, her back flush against his chest, giggling each time he whispers in her ear. When he pulls a throw blanket over their laps, everything in me stills.

My brain screams at me to leave, to hide behind the closed door of my bedroom, but I'm rooted to the spot. The agony of watching him kiss her neck as his hands wander over her body is too much.

My heart thrashes against my rib cage, and unwanted heat coils low in my gut.

I should look away.

I should leave.

But I don't.

While Logan sneaks his hand under the blanket and nibbles on her throat, I study her face. Her features tense, her brows pulling together. Eyes falling closed, she sucks in a breath and arches into him.

Holy shit.

I don't need to see what he's doing under the blanket to know she's unraveling for him right there, inches from me.

When a soft moan escapes her lips, I look away. No matter how much it tears me apart, I don't want them to stop. I want to know what she sounds like when she comes. I want to know what she looks like.

And this is the only way I'll ever know. By watching my best friend pleasure her.

Something inside me cracks. I can't make sense of it. It's like for the first time since my granny died, the emptiness I've been dragging around, the grief I've been carrying, twists into raw hunger. Pure need.

It's so much more than simple desire. The sensation overtaking me is the need to possess her.

Despite the way my cock thickens, shame washes over me.

What the fuck? What's wrong with me? I shouldn't want her. She's Logan's. She deserves better than the wreck I am, and my best friend is perfect for her.

I clench my jaw, grinding my molars together, and force myself to look away. If I don't, I'll do something reckless, and there will be no coming back from it.

But my chest won't stop aching. My fingers itch to touch her again. My body craves hers. I can't stop myself from imagining what it would be like to taste her. Holding my breath, I fight the urge. If I give in, I won't be soft. I'll demolish everything around me with a force that will destroy my friendship with Logan, and I can't let that happen.

Her quiet whimper sends a shiver down my spine. No matter how hard I fight it, my body takes over, and when I turn, time freezes, and a wave of scorching heat washes over me.

Because this time, I'm not the only one watching.

This time, she's watching me too.

## EIGHT

# I Want Both of You

YANA

I HOLD CAMDEN'S GAZE AS LOGAN LEAVES A TRAIL OF kisses along my throat and rubs my clit between his fingers. My mind is foggy as overwhelming pleasure builds inside me, but I can't make myself look away from the dark-haired man sitting no more than four feet away.

And he's watching me too.

Fire burns hot in my chest, wild and reckless. Before I can think better of it, I lean away from Logan, halting his caress, and slide my hand off the couch. When I catch Camden's wrist, his skin nearly burns me.

Eyes widening, he examines me.

"Yana..." Logan murmurs in my ear, voice low but steady.

Without letting go of Camden's wrist, I meet Logan's gaze. He searches my face, eyes intense. What strikes me is that he doesn't look angry or even surprised. The corners of his mouth tip up, and his expression turns knowing, understanding, like he's been waiting for this moment to happen.

"You sure about this?" he asks me. "I know I am, but I want you to be certain too."

"I'm sure," I whisper. "I want both of you."

A beautiful smile curves his lips, and he nods. Then he fixes his focus on Camden. "You heard her. Are you in?"

Camden stares, confusion swimming in his eyes like he doesn't believe us.

I tug on his hand, shaking him out of his stupor, silently urging him to make a decision. There's no way I'm the only one who felt like my body was on fire after I bumped into him on my way to the kitchen. His heart was ready to jump out of his chest then, and now his pulse is hammering under my fingers.

Slowly, he sets his bottle on the floor. Then he rises onto his knees in front of me, his expression full of hope and uncertainty. "Are you sure?"

Logan chuckles softly behind me. "Yes, we are." In one quick movement, he yanks the throw blanket off my lap.

I slide closer to the edge of the couch, my knees on either side of Camden's hips. Holding his gaze, I lean in. "Stop pretending you don't want me."

He clenches his jaw, his eyes burning into mine. "You have no idea what I want."

A breathy huff leaves me, half desire, half irritation. "Then prove me wrong."

"Fuck," he mutters. Sliding his hand around the back of my neck, he pulls me into him and covers my lips with his.

The kiss is rough and desperate. His teeth sink into my bottom lip, making me gasp. Taking advantage of the moment, he slips his tongue into my mouth and curls it around mine. Instantly, the moment is hot and heavy. He's not holding back.

Logan cups my breast from behind, squeezing it roughly and making my vision blur. The pleasure is almost unbearable.

With his mouth near my ear, he rasps, "That's right, Cam. Take what you want."

I moan into Camden's mouth. I'm losing my mind, caught between these two men. Logan plays with my nipples through my shirt, tugging and pulling in all the right ways, while Camden holds me close, as if he's afraid I'll slip away if he doesn't.

The moment feels like a dream. I never back away from what I want, and because of my career and my life experiences, I prefer to be direct, to show my interest and talk about my needs from the start. Yet I've never imagined myself being with two men at the same time. Surely, I can blame it on the alcohol, on being trapped here like this, but I don't make a habit of deluding myself. I've been attracted to Logan *and* Camden from the very beginning, despite the latter being a jerk to me that first day.

The need coursing through me is all-consuming. I never want it to stop.

Camden grips my hips and pulls me closer. The move makes Logan shift forward. When my back is glued to his chest again, his hardness pokes into my ass.

"Easy," he murmurs. "Don't break her, man."

"She's not made of glass," Camden whispers against my lips.

"I'm definitely not," I breathe.

Camden rears back, his eyes searching mine. He takes a few deep breaths, as if trying to steady himself.

Logan caresses my tits with slow and gentle movements.

The heat in my core turns molten. Shit. I'm so turned on, I can't even think straight.

"Take off her leggings," Logan says, his tone firm and commanding. He's enjoying this way more than I expected.

The words send a shiver through me.

Camden swallows, his Adam's apple moving up and down. His lips are swollen from our kisses, and it only makes him look more gorgeous. "If I do this...I don't think I'll be able to stop."

"I don't want you to," I whisper with a hand pressed to his chest. "Neither of you."

The fireplace crackles, throwing shadows across the room. The movie continues to play, like a soundtrack to the moment. Wind rattles the windows slightly, a storm raging outside while another one burns between us.

Logan shifts and bands his arms around me, kissing the side of my neck, his movements slow, deliberate, while Camden slides his hands up my legs, his eyes dark and hungry.

I'm totally at their mercy. Trapped between them, the heat from their skin sets my own on fire. Camden tugs on the waistband of my leggings, and I lift my ass so he can peel them down, along with my panties. As he tosses them to the side, he zeroes in on my pussy, firelight flickering in his irises.

"Spread your legs for him." Logan hooks my right leg over his, then does the same with my left.

My chest heaves. I'm fully exposed, but instead of fear or shame, the emotion growing stronger inside me is pure desire. My need for these two men is nearly unbearable.

"Look at him, Queen. Look him in the eye. Show him how much you want this." Logan slides his hand lower, trapping my clit between his thumb and index finger and slowly circling it.

After the way he's been edging me and the need Camden's kisses ignited, I won't last long. I hold Camden's gaze as Logan rubs my clit, relishing the warmth that's pooling in my lower abdomen. As my breathing turns shallow, Camden tightens his jaw.

Logan works me over faster, his fingers expertly flicking over my clit.

"*Bozhe, I seichas konchu.*[1]" Eyes rolling back, I drop my head against Logan's shoulder. An intense shudder works its way through my body, and my orgasm takes over. Eyes still on Camden's, I groan.

The sound is cut off when Logan cups my face and slams his lips to mine.

When my body stops trembling, he releases my mouth, and when I open my eyes, I find Camden still watching me, riveted. His fists are clenched at his sides, like he's barely holding himself back.

In this moment, I know it's not the end of the night. Not even close.

Brows pinched together, Camden grabs my hips and draws me closer. The sensation of his calloused hands on my sensitive skin sends

---

1. God, I'm gonna come.

a thrill of excitement through me. He places a soft, surprisingly gentle kiss on my inner thigh before sinking his teeth into the flesh, leaving a mark. He moves up, all lips, tongue, and teeth, setting my every nerve ending alight. I feel everything, and it's exhilarating.

Logan cups my tits from behind, sucking on the sensitive skin of my neck, then lapping over the place he bit.

It's a miracle, really, that I'm still conscious and coherent because these men are driving me out of my mind.

"Fuck..." Camden mutters against my thigh. "You don't even know what you're doing to me."

"Then show me," I whisper, practically vibrating with anticipation.

Logan's breath is warm against my ear. "Don't keep her waiting, Cam."

I should be overwhelmed, torn apart by the storm I've found myself in the middle of. Instead, this feels inevitable. Like I was always meant to end up here, trapped between Logan's steadiness and Camden's wildfire.

When Camden's hot breath fans over my clit, I arch into him, desperate to feel his lips on my pussy. When his eyes find mine, he smirks, and before I know it, he's lapping over my soft spot. He alternates between licking and sucking, driving me higher and higher, and when he drags his teeth over my clit, my vision goes dark. I have to brace myself against Logan to keep from going completely boneless.

"Fuck, Red," Camden growls, his voice rough. "You taste like you were made to ruin me."

With a hand in his hair, I tug and twist. He groans and doubles down. I respond with a moan that echoes off the high ceiling, rolling my hips.

It's fucking heaven. No doubt about it.

Logan kisses my cheek and the corner of my mouth, steadying me. Grounding me. Giving me something to hold on to when my second orgasm of the night slams into me. I shatter from head to toe, trembling uncontrollably in Logan's arms while Camden continues his assault. It's like he's been starving for years and has only now found a way to satisfy his hunger.

When my orgasm ebbs, I sag against Logan's chest. Breathing heavily, I open my eyes and find Camden's locked on my face. The devilish smile that plays on his lips makes me dizzy.

The fire is still crackling. The storm still howls against the cabin walls, but none of us speaks.

There's no going back from what we just did. And yet, none of us stopped it.

"*Bozhe*," I mumble, covering my face with one hand. "That was fucking amazing, but...this isn't fair. Why am I the one getting all the attention?"

Logan snorts, his chest vibrating with laughter.

"You don't get it, do you?" Camden lets out a sardonic laugh, then shakes his head.

He scoops me into his arms and stands.

Instinctively, I cling to him as he strides down the hallway. "What are you doing?"

"Shut up, Red," he all but growls.

"Better do as he tells you." Logan's mischievous voice signals that he isn't far behind.

Camden eases me onto the bed and guides me to the middle. Then he stretches out on my left side while Logan lounges on my right.

In a matter of minutes, the three of us are a tangle of limbs and heat. There's no rush, no roughness. It's all about slow kisses and lingering touches, the experience soft but no less charged. Logan trails his lips down my jaw; Camden presses his palm to my cheek, kissing me like he doesn't know whether to hold me close or push me away. I melt into them. With their hands and lips on my skin, with their attention fixed solely on me, I turn into an incoherent mess.

Eventually, exhaustion wins. Our kisses turn lazy, our touches featherlight.

I curl into Logan's chest, his steady warmth cocooning me as he wraps his arm around my shoulders.

Just as my eyelids grow heavy and sleep threatens to pull me under, the mattress shifts.

Eyes half open, I turn and spy a silhouette hovering beside the bed in the darkness. Camden sits on the edge, his head in his hands, his shoulders tense.

I reach over, but before I can touch him, he stands.

My chest aches, and my throat gets painfully tight.

Without looking at me, without looking at Logan, he silently creeps out of the room and shuts the door behind him.

A sharp pain ripples through my heart. I want to call after him, ask him why he left and beg him to stay. Instead, I force myself to relax against Logan, sinking deeper into the warmth of his body, and let sleep win.

Tomorrow is a new day, and I will talk to him. If Camden thinks I won't be asking questions, he's wrong.

NINE

# Only if It's with You

LOGAN

I OPEN MY EYES, TAKING A MOMENT TO ENJOY THE FEELING of Yana's warm body pressed against mine. She's curled into me, her hair spilling over her pillow, her face relaxed. Fuck, I could stay like this all day. A smile grows on my lips as images from last night appear in my mind. My body heats, the blood in my veins like a sizzling fire.

Our encounter was mind-blowing.

It probably should've felt wrong. Instead, it felt incredibly right. Making Yana come while Camden watched every flick of my fingers over her clit, and then watching him kiss her and eat her out? I've never been more turned on than I was yesterday, especially when Cam brought her into her room and the three of us ended up tangled together.

It was like my world clicked into place. Like that was exactly how it should've been from the start. Yana, Camden, and me. I didn't feel even an ounce of jealousy. The moment she reached for him, I knew that if I was going to share her with anyone, it could only be him—my best friend.

Slowly, I lift my head, searching for him, only to find his side of the bed empty. A niggle of disappointment threads through me.

I ease out of bed, doing my best not to jostle Yana, and check the time. When I realize it's only eight, my eyebrows hit my hairline. Why is he up so early?

On silent feet, I head to the bathroom to wash my face and relieve myself, then I pad to the kitchen.

Camden is leaning against the counter with a mug in his hand, dressed in a black hoodie and sweatpants, his hair a mess. His eyes are locked on mine, but he doesn't greet me. He doesn't smile either.

Unease replaces disappointment. What's gotten into him?

"Merry Christmas," I say, reaching for a mug in the cupboard.

"Uh-huh," he grumbles in response. "There's coffee if you want."

"Thanks."

I fill my cup and prop my hip against the counter, studying him. He looks the opposite of how I feel. While I'm exhilarated, excited, he looks gloomy and closed off.

But why?

"How long have you been up?" I ask, deciding to go easy on him instead of interrogating him.

"Ten minutes."

I blink. "But when I woke up—"

"I slept in my room."

Confusion joins the sensations swirling in my head. "Why?"

He chuckles dryly. "Do I really need to spell it out for you?"

"That'd be great, yeah, because I don't get it."

"You and Yana are together. And I'm the third wheel."

I lower my mug to the counter without even taking a sip. "Are you seriously telling me you feel like a third wheel after what happened last night?"

"And what exactly happened last night?" he snaps. "We all got drunk, and things got out of hand. Forced proximity and all that shit."

"We were drinking, but none of us were *drunk*. We all knew what we were doing," I tell him, ducking in hopes of snagging his attention.

"Really?" he huffs. "You would've shared your girl with me if you were sober?"

I push off the counter, step in front of him, and hold eye contact.

"With you—yes. You are my best friend. I've known you my whole life. I trust you. It only could've happened with you."

He sets his mug on the counter, then pushes past me, pacing the room. "You have no idea what you're talking about."

"I know you want her. You've wanted her since the night we met her," I say, my voice even. "Why are you running away from your feelings?"

He halts in his tracks and whips around to face me, his mouth twisting. "Don't start, Logan."

"I'm not starting anything. I'm telling it like it is. You wanted to be there. So why did you walk out?"

"Maybe because I don't like being a charity case," he grits out.

"Please." I snort. "We weren't taking pity on you, and you know that. You're not as discreet as you think you are, buddy. I saw the way you looked at her, how badly you wanted her. She wanted you too, and I had nothing against it."

He throws his head back and laughs darkly. "How generous of you. But have you stopped to think that maybe I don't need your permission?" He narrows his eyes. "Aren't you worried that she might be more into me than you? That she might cast you aside?"

The jab hits hard, but I tamp down my irritation and grin instead. His defensiveness is hilarious. He can try to dismiss the desire all he wants, but there's no denying it. All three of us felt it last night.

"No." I shrug. "I'm not. Yesterday was fucking perfect. I'm not opposed to the idea of sharing her. If that's what *she* wants. And only if it's with you."

He stares at me like I've lost my mind, his jaw rigid. Then he slips his fingers into his hair, tugging at the roots. "Jesus Christ, Logan, do you even hear yourself? You don't share a woman like her."

"Why not? *She* wanted it. Yana initiated everything," I shoot back. "Isn't that what's most important?"

For a split second, fire flickers in his eyes, but he douses it almost immediately. "You're insane," he mutters, rushing to the front door. He stuffs his feet into his shoes, snags his jacket, and slams the door behind him.

In the silent aftermath, I let out a slow breath and drag a hand down my face. That conversation didn't go the way I thought it would. Not even close. Damn him and his stubbornness. Why does he have to make everything complicated?

With another exhale, I open the fridge. I pull out a carton of eggs and a package of bacon and turn to the stove. If nothing else, Yana deserves to wake up to breakfast.

I'M LEANING against the counter, a mug of freshly brewed coffee in hand, when Yana wanders into the kitchen. Her hair's in a messy bun, and she's dressed in black leggings and a red T-shirt. Eyes still sleepy, she smiles when she catches me watching her. "How long have you been up?"

I glance at the clock on the wall. "Half an hour or so."

She steps into me and buries her face in my chest. "Good morning," she whispers. "And Merry Christmas."

"Morning." I drop my lips to her forehead. "I made breakfast and coffee."

She leans away, beaming. "So now you cook?"

"For you? Of course."

As we eat, she asks about my family and how we celebrate Christmas. The conversation is light and sweet, but I can't go any longer without mentioning last night and Camden's reaction this morning.

"So, about last night..." I trail off, my pulse picking up. "Are we good?"

With a genuine smile, she nods. "More than good. I don't regret it. Not for a second." She bites her bottom lip nervously, but she doesn't look away. "I'm attracted to him too. To Camden. I think I've been attracted to him since the night I met you both."

I nod despite the little pang in my chest. She met him first, technically. It's hard not to wonder what would have happened if Camden hadn't made that rude comment at the restaurant. If he'd approached her first.

Would I be here? Would he be so willing to share her with me if he were in my place?

"Logan?" Yana covers my hand with hers. Her brows knit together, and her lips part slightly. "Are *we* good?"

I give her a reassuring smile. "Of course we are. If I weren't okay with it, I wouldn't have let it go that far." I thread my fingers through hers. "And I could tell you were into him too. Just like he's obviously into you." I lick my lips. "But he walked out. I tried talking to him this morning, and he just...left."

Head tilted, she studies me. Then, with a shrug of one shoulder, she says, "Then I guess I'll have to talk some sense into him."

I chuckle. "Good luck. He was in a mood when he stormed out."

With a wink, she stands and starts gathering dishes.

I stand too, taking them from her. "Go. Find him. I'll take care of this. Then I need to call my family."

"You're the best." She kisses me on the lips, sweet and slow. Then she heads down the hall to her room.

A few minutes later, when she walks out the front door wearing black leggings, a white hoodie, and a jacket, I'm not concerned. The unease I felt this morning is gone, and all that's left is anticipation.

TEN

# Such a Good Boy

CAMDEN

As the biting wind assaults my cheeks, I adjust my hood. *Fuck*. The cold slips through my jacket and my hoodie, making me shiver as I trudge along the snowy trail back to the cabin.

I thought a walk would clear my head. It didn't. If anything, I'm more wound up than I was almost an hour ago, when I stormed outside.

Logan's words keep echoing in my head, as if they're lyrics to a song stuck on repeat. *I'm not opposed to the idea of sharing her. If that's what she wants. And only if it's with you.*

The suggestion is wrong on so many levels. It shouldn't sit right with me. Yet it does. It fucking does because last night felt too damn good. Too natural. And now it's too easy to imagine it happening again. And again. And again.

And that's the problem.

No matter what he says now, once we leave this snow-globe fantasy, reality will come crashing back down. And in reality, Logan and Yana are a couple. A fucking perfect match. Me? I'm the sidekick. A third wheel, and I'll be all alone again the moment this snowed-in dream ends.

That's the story of my life. Camden Hayes, the guy no one needs. I'm an afterthought. After losing my parents and then my granny, who was my whole world, I won't survive watching Yana and Logan continue on together without me. Not after this. Not after I had a taste.

Dammit, I should've gone to bed last night. I shouldn't have let it happen.

By the time the cabin comes into view in the distance, the storm brewing in my chest is as violent as the one last night.

And that's when I see her. Yana, walking toward me, bundled up in a jacket, her hair catching snowflakes in a messy bun.

"Hey," she says softly as she approaches.

I stop in my tracks and force a nod, slipping my hands in my pockets and curling them into fists. "Hey."

"Merry Christmas, Camden."

"Thanks." I swallow thickly, my throat suddenly dry. "I suppose I can't really wish *you* a merry Christmas, can I?"

"You can. People always say it back to me, and I usually don't correct them." She smiles at me, her eyes sparkling. "Are you heading back inside?"

"Yeah," I huff, my breath forming a cloud between us. "It's colder out here than I expected." And the walk was useless. I'm still as riled up as I was when I left the cabin, if not more.

She nibbles her bottom lip. "Mind if I join you?"

Snorting, I hold out an arm, gesturing to the forest around us. "We're in the middle of nowhere. You really think I'd be against having your company?"

"Maybe I was counting on it." She winks at me, and the tension in my muscles melts a little.

We fall into step, snow crunching under our shoes. It's a short walk back to the cabin, but I'm grateful for even these crumbs of her time. Fuck, I'm desperate...and delusional. What a combination.

"How do you usually celebrate Christmas and New Year's?" she asks.

"I've always celebrated with my granny." I suck in a breath. "But last year I spent the holidays alone. Logan's family has invited me to visit anytime I want, but..." I scratch at my jaw. "I don't know."

"It's great that the two of you have such a strong friendship. I have a lot of friends at home, but my best friend is close with my family too, so I get it."

She's trying to lighten up the mood, encouraging me to open up. Instead, all she's done is push me even closer to the edge. My head is pounding, and my heartbeat thunders in my throat.

"You don't know me," I grumble.

"Well, yeah. That's why I'm trying to *get* to know you."

Anger coils in my stomach. Why won't she just let this shit go? "There's no need."

She grasps my arm and stops, turning to me. "I know what you're doing."

I should go back inside. Keep my distance. But I can't make myself leave her side. So I turn to face her. "And what am I doing?"

Her gray-green eyes narrow on me. "Pushing me away. Building a wall between us."

Pain lances my chest, sharp and quick. "That's because it's the right thing to do."

Brow arched, she folds her arms over her chest. "Says who?"

"Me." I clench my jaw. "You're with my friend. End of story."

"Can't I have a say in it?"

I scrub a hand down my face, the warmth of my palm a shock. "I don't think so. Did you forget that I'm an asshole?"

"Last night, I swore I saw something under this whole 'I'm a superficial jerk' exterior." She looks me up and down. "Apparently, I was wrong."

She turns away, but before she can continue on, I grab her hand, stopping her. "You. Don't. Know. Me," I tell her.

Our faces are inches apart. The proximity sends a zing of excitement down my spine, loosening the knot my gut was twisted into. At least a little. "I noticed you first. Me, not Logan."

Eyes flaring, she yanks free of my hold. "Then why didn't you say something? Why were you so damn rude?"

"Because that's what I do, Yana." I bristle, my defenses kicking in. "I push people away before they have a chance to do it for me." My voice is sharper than I mean for it to be. "And you—God, you were too much. Too beautiful for a guy like me. Too fucking bright."

"Nice try. You only said something after you heard me talking to Roman. It was your insecurities speaking."

"What insecurities?" I wave a hand between us. "You came to our table and ignored the whole team, then started speaking in Russian. It was disrespectful."

Head thrown back, she lets out a laugh. "I didn't greet the team because Roman intercepted me before I got the chance. He stood up to talk to me. And you threw a tantrum because we had a two-minute conversation you couldn't understand. That says a lot about your insecurities and about how much you value the opinions of others."

My chest squeezes. "What fucking bullshit."

"No. It's not." Chin lifted, she locks eyes with me. "Who cares what other people think? Who cares what they say? Why are you giving someone else's opinion so much power? This is stupid." She steps closer, her chest rising and falling rapidly. "I could switch to Russian right now and badmouth you all I want. I'd use the sweetest tone, and you wouldn't understand me. That shouldn't offend you. My words hold no weight. My opinion doesn't matter. That's how it should be. Especially when someone says something you *do* understand." She pokes my chest with her finger. "And now you're telling me that you noticed me first, like I should feel bad about talking to Logan when he approached me that night. But that's on you. Not on me, not on Logan. On *you*. Grow up, Camden. Being this salty is not sexy at all."

I'm fucking fuming. Not only because every word she uttered is true, but also because I want her even more than I did a moment ago. Before I can second-guess myself, I grab her wrist, pull her into me, and slam my mouth to hers.

The kiss is wild. It's teeth and heat and all the feelings I've been holding back. She kisses me back just as fiercely. I clutch her to my chest, and she fists my jacket. She traces my bottom lip with her tongue, asking for permission, and I let her in. Our tongues tangle and twirl around each other. I'm no longer cold. I'm fucking burning.

A moan escapes her, instantly sobering me up. Reality slams back into me, and I tear myself away from her, my chest heaving. "This is a mistake," I mutter.

Her puffy lips part as she gapes at me. Then she blinks, a frown etched onto her face. "*Idi na huyi*[1], Camden."

She spins around and stomps toward the cabin.

I should let her leave. It's the right thing to do, but with every foot of space she puts between us, the ache in my chest intensifies. Fucking hell.

With a growl, I take off after her. I catch up just as she approaches her car and grasp her elbow, causing her to stagger back.

She yanks her arm away, trying to break free from my grip, but I slip an arm around her torso and press her to my chest.

With my mouth at her ear, I grit out, "Don't walk away from me."

"Let me go," she hisses.

With a grunt, I turn her around and push her against her car, then hover so close we're breathing the same air. I don't know who moves first, but suddenly, we're kissing again. Even harder and wilder than the last time. We battle for dominance, my tongue against hers. I devour her every whimper, every sound she makes.

She fists my jacket and tugs me closer, leaving no space between us. I slide my hands down her ass and lift her, pressing her against the car door, and with her legs wrapped around my hips, she grinds her center over my hard-on.

"I want you," I confess, nibbling on her bottom lip.

"Keys...in my pocket."

I put her down and take a step back so she can dig them out, and in the space of a few heartbeats, we're both in the back seat. She lies on her back, and I hover over her, nestled between her legs, with my hands planted on either side of her.

Our lips are still fused, our tongues playing cat and mouse as I roll my hips, searching for friction, and she continues grinding her core against me.

---

1. Go fuck yourself

It's like we're trying to consume each other.

"*Ty svodish menya s uma*[2]," she whispers as I suck on her neck.

I have no idea what she just said, but I want to beg her to keep talking because just the sound of her voice makes me see stars.

I lean away, taking in her flushed cheeks and her hooded eyes. "I want you," I tell her again.

Breaking into a seductive smile, she unzips her jacket. "Then take me."

With shaking hands, I take off my jacket. Then I help her out of hers. The back seat of her car isn't the most comfortable place to fuck, but I don't care. All I want is to bury my cock deep inside her.

She scoots away a couple of inches and slips off her leggings and panties, shuddering against the cold.

Angling to the side, I slam the door closed. Then I push my own sweatpants lower and sit. I hiss when I make contact with the icy leather seat.

"My ass is fucking freezing." I chuckle.

"Poor Camden. We can't have that, can we?" she purrs as she climbs onto my lap. With her attention fixed on my cock, she wraps her fingers around it and gives it a gentle squeeze. "So smooth...and long..."

Smirking, I grip her hips. "I bet it will fit perfectly inside your warm pussy."

"I bet it will." She hoists herself up and guides my dick to her entrance. With her hands on my shoulders, she slides down my shaft, taking me inside her inch by inch. "*O bozhe*[3]," she moans when I'm fully seated, her eyes falling closed.

"Fuck," I rasp. "You feel so good."

She hovers closer and captures my lips with hers. Hips rolling, she rides me, her movements slow and gentle at first. We kiss and kiss, coming up for air for a moment before we devour each other again. If we keep this up, her lips will become my addiction.

---

2. You drive me insane
3. Oh God

"You're taking me so well, baby," I murmur, tightening my hold and rocking her over my lap.

She picks up the pace, her movements becoming more urgent, more frenzied, and rides me with abandon, her moans and whimpers filling the car. I sink my fingers deeper into her flesh. With every dip of her hips, the fire forming in my lower abdomen grows stronger. I'll be coming in no time, but I don't want to do it before her.

We're like fire and gasoline, burning hot, even in this freezing SUV. The sound of skin slapping against skin fills the space as she fucks me harder and rougher than before, nearly making me lose control.

"Fuck, Red...I'm gonna come..." I growl, biting on her bottom lip.

"Then come. Shoot your load inside me," she whimpers, her inner walls clenching hard enough to pull my orgasm from me.

"Fuck." I spill inside her, my head thrown back, every muscle tensing.

"*Horoshiyi mal'chik.*[4]" Moaning, she spasms around me, and when her own muscles relax, she buries her face in the crook of my neck and moves her hips lazily, prolonging her release and making me feel like I'm in heaven. With the memory of the way she tastes fresh in my mind and her nails digging into my shoulders, I've never felt better. My every cell vibrates with want. No regret. No shame. Just want—because I want more.

As we fumble back into our clothes, we laugh and smile, and before she climbs out of the car, I steal another kiss.

"Who would've thought you could be so obedient?" Yana teases as we amble toward the cabin. "You were such a good boy."

I snort. "Is that what you said to me while you were coming?"

Her eyes twinkle. "Maybe."

Fuck, I can barely keep my hands to myself. With her cheeks flushed and her lips swollen, she's even harder to resist. All I can think about is pulling her back against me and getting started on round two.

---

4. Good boy

I guide her into the cabin, and we're instantly hit with the heat of the fireplace. We're hit with a shit-eating grin from Logan, too. He's sitting on the couch. *Elf* is playing on the TV, but he's examining us with an amused glint in his eye.

"Well," he drawls, "you could've invited me too."

Maybe I should be ashamed. Maybe I should panic about getting caught. Instead, a smug smile overtakes me.

"Maybe next time." I wink at him.

At that, my best friend bursts into laughter.

## ELEVEN

# Only Ours

YANA

The kitchen smells incredible. Like roasted chicken, garlic, onions, tangerine, and the dressing for the salad I threw together. Camden's at the stove, wearing nothing but low-slung sweatpants, stirring the sauce like he's a contestant on a damn cooking show. I'm not exactly sure what his goal is—to make a perfect mushroom cream sauce or to make me horny. Right now, horniness is winning out.

"Has anyone ever told you, Red, that you're bossy?" he mutters. "It's just sauce. Stop acting like we're cooking for a Michelin-starred restaurant."

"This may not be a fancy restaurant, but the sauce is for our Christmas dinner, so it should be perfect." I sidle up beside him, my shoulder brushing his.

Smiling, he shakes his head, a sense of ease rolling off him.

Logan hums "Last Christmas" while he chops vegetables, way too pleased with himself. I wander over to him and steal a cherry tomato from under the knife.

"Hey!" He turns to look at me, eyebrows pulled together. "Behave yourself. I could have cut you."

I bump my hip against his. "I'm the queen. Have you forgotten? I can do anything I want."

Chuckling, he tips his chin to Camden. "Looks like being with both of us has gone to her head, don't you think?"

Camden flexes one arm, making his muscles bulge. "Have you seen us, man? We're catches, and she snared us both. Red has every reason to be smug."

I tap my bottom lip. "'Red' and 'Queen'? Suddenly, I feel like a character from *Alice in Wonderland*."

"What does that make us, then?" Logan snakes an arm around my waist and pulls me to his side. The heat of his naked chest sends a delicious thrill down my spine.

"Good question. If I'm a queen, who are you?" I tease as I melt into him.

Snickering, Camden turns off the stove. "Your kings. Obviously."

"What he said." Logan kisses my temple.

I slip out of his hold, pick up the Olivier salad, and wander to the dining table. The Russian potato salad is a holiday staple in my family. I'm thousands of miles away, but making the familiar side dish makes me feel like I'm carrying a piece of home with me.

I can't stop myself from smiling when I return to the kitchen and find Logan popping a spoonful of the sauce Camden made into his mouth.

"That's good," he says. "I didn't know you could cook like that."

"I can't." Camden shoots me a look, eyes burning into mine. "It's only good because of Yana's guidance."

"Ah. Makes sense." Logan sighs. "She makes everything perfect."

"Flattery will get you everywhere." I waggle my brows at him, then meet Camden's gaze. "Both of you actually."

The man with the dark, messy hair gives me a smoldering look. "I think I speak for us both when I say your bed is the only place we want to be."

Snorting, I pick up the plate of roasted chicken. "I never would have guessed you'd be so cheesy."

"Me neither, dude." Logan claps Camden on the shoulder as he picks up a stack of plates.

"If you prefer my default version, when I'm a total asshole, just let me know," Camden taunts as he adds the sauce to the mashed potatoes.

"Don't you fucking dare." Logan barks out a laugh, following me out of the room.

CANDLES FLICKER, causing shadows to dance on the walls around us. Our plates are clean, and the second bottle of red wine is half empty. Jokes and conversations are flowing, and my mood is lighter than it's been in months. Maybe a year. All thanks to these two men and the atmosphere they create.

"Remember how my mom always bakes cookies on Christmas Eve?" Logan asks Camden. "And how she always ends up burning at least a dozen of them?"

"She may ruin the first batch, but the rest are delicious." Shrugging, Camden lifts his glass to his lips. "They never last more than a day or two."

Logan laughs. "That's the truth. Lucy loves them the most. She's literally bribed Dad and me to share our cookies all her life."

"She suckered me into it a few times too," Camden adds, giving my knee a gentle squeeze. "I never say no to your little sister. Hell, she's practically my little sister too."

"Yeah, she loves you, and so do my parents. You should come with me the next time I fly home." Logan drapes his arm over the back of my chair and traces his finger over my shoulder. "Don't shut us out, Cam, please."

"I won't." He nods, his lips pressed into a straight line. "That's actually what my granny told me, not long before she..." He sighs and swallows thickly. "She reminded me that even though I might not have any blood relatives left, the Reid family will always welcome me like one of their own."

"We will. You're like a brother to me."

Tears prick at the backs of my eyes, and a wave of warmth spreads through my body, filling me with happiness. It's so good to see them bond like this, to witness the way they're opening up to each other.

"Hey, Queen?" Logan leans closer, wiping a tear that escaped without my permission. "Is everything okay?"

"More than okay. I'm happy for you. It's like this was meant to be. You two were meant to be stuck together like this so you could really talk to each other. Without secrets."

"You're right. This snowed-in situation really brought us closer." Logan sighs, then looks at Camden. "You know what I miss about your granny?"

A loud snort springs out of Camden's mouth. "Her pierogies?"

"Damn right." Logan crosses an ankle over his knee. "They were delicious."

I peer over at Camden, my elbows on the table. "Pierogies? Was your granny Polish?"

"She was. She moved to the US from Kraków when she was eighteen. Her name was Katarzyna, but my grandpa always called her Kasia. He was American, and he loved her more than anything."

"Have you ever been to Poland?"

"No." He shakes his head, ducking a little. "But I always wanted to."

I grin at Camden, then at Logan. "We should go. I've been to Poland so many times. I've seen almost everything there is to see, and I love it. I'd be happy to go with you."

"Great idea." Camden smiles warmly at me. Then he fixes his focus on Logan. "Will you come with us?"

"Ha. As if I'd ever leave you two alone any longer than I had to."

"Afraid of a little competition?" Camden angles in and quirks an eyebrow.

Logan lifts a shoulder in an easy shrug. "Nope, because there is no competition. And it's not our call to make anyway. If Yana wants us both, she wants us both. And I, for one, am okay with that."

"Works for me." Camden gives my knee another gentle squeeze. "What about your family? Any holiday traditions?"

"Yeah, other than the Olivier salad?" Logan drags his fingers in circles over my skin.

The fire their touches have ignited within me grows stronger. It heats my skin and makes my center throb.

When Camden notices the way I'm clenching my legs together, he gives me a smug smile.

Cheeky asshole.

"Well." I clear my throat. "We used to decorate the tree on December 24th. Mom says that it creates a magical atmosphere and helps to prepare for the New Year. It adds to the experience. Dad always hid candies between the branches. It drove Mom nuts. We don't do the whole stocking thing, and we don't have any elves on shelves. This one confused the hell out of me the first time I heard about it, but I think I kind of get it now. We do have a Ded Moroz—he's like our version of Santa Claus. And we typically wake up on January 1st and open gifts."

"Does your family eat anything else as incredible as the Olivier salad?" Logan asks, bringing his glass to his lips.

"Mashed potatoes, bread with caviar, homemade pickles, along with two or three salads my mom makes. But the best part has always been my granny's Napoleon cake. It's literally the most delicious dessert I've ever had. No matter what I eat or where I eat it, her cake will always be the food I love the most."

"Nice." Logan smiles. "I hope one day I can try all that too."

"Same," Camden chimes in.

The adoration in their expressions causes heat to creep into my cheeks. And as weird as it sounds, making plans, the three of us, feels absurdly normal. It feels right. Like I belong with these two men who I've only known for a couple of days. Like this is exactly how it should be.

After we've cleaned up and the dishes are done, I lie on the fluffy rug in front of the fireplace with Logan on my right side and Camden on my left, talking about anything and everything—practices, tournaments, countries we've visited.

Until Logan turns and props his head on his knuckles, his focus on me suddenly intense.

"What?" I ask, my pulse skyrocketing.

"We're leaving tomorrow."

"Yeah."

Camden mirrors Logan, peering down at me. "And what are we going to do once we leave?"

I bite my bottom lip and consider what I want and how this could work, but I'm being put on the spot. I've been living in the moment, not worrying about the future. Not yet. So I say, "I don't want to choose. I like you both, a lot. If you think we can make this work, I'd be more than willing to try."

While they assess each other, quietly communicating, I wait, nervous and excited at the same time.

"Like I said this morning," Logan murmurs, "if I'm going to share her, it'd only be with you. We make a great team, on and off the ice, and I have a feeling it'll be even better in bed with this gorgeous woman between us."

Camden chews on his bottom lip, hesitation in his eyes.

My heart leaps into my throat, and I clench my jaw tight. It will hurt a shit ton if he says—

A low rumble of laughter escapes him, leaving me stunned. What the hell?

"I see the fear in your eyes, Red. Did you really think I'd say no?" Cam looks from me to Logan and back again. "I've never felt more alive than when I'm with you. It doesn't matter if I'm sharing you with my best friend or fucking you in the back seat of your car. I want you, and I don't want you to have to choose. Or maybe..." He hovers closer, his hair falling over his forehead. "I want you to choose us both."

"Always," I whisper.

"Then you're ours now." He places his lips on mine, kissing me softly. "Only ours."

Once Camden pulls back, Logan takes my hand and helps me to

my feet. He lifts me into his arms and carries me bridal style down the hall to my bedroom.

Camden follows a moment later, having switched off the gas fireplace.

The two of them stand in front of me as I sit on the bed. Shoulder to shoulder, dressed in nothing but sweatpants. Eyes darkening with desire, they study me as if I'm their prey...but also something precious.

They are admiring me.

"A little Christmas present for us, maybe?" Logan teases.

"The best Christmas present I've ever gotten." Camden breaks into a sinful smile and drops to his knees. "One I plan to devour tonight."

"I think you meant to say *we*." Logan sits beside me on the bed and cups my cheek with his big, calloused hand.

"Definitely we." Camden plants a kiss on my knee. "Because she's ours."

As Logan pulls me in for a kiss, Camden works my leggings down my hips. Instantly, all my senses are on high alert, and anticipation courses through my veins.

In this moment, I think I understand what magic really feels like.

TWELVE

# It's a Choice

LOGAN

IT'S DIFFERENT TONIGHT. NO EXCUSES, NO PRETENDING this is a one-time slip we'll laugh about later. It's us, pure fire and passion, but also care and tenderness. It's Yana and Camden and me, and the more I think about the night we met, the more certain I am that we were inevitable. It feels too right.

Camden is on his knees between Yana's legs, licking and sucking and lapping at her clit.

Still sitting beside her, I drink her in, relishing the ecstasy on her face. Her eyes are half-closed, her lips parted, her eyebrows knitting together and then relaxing.

It's the most beautiful thing I've ever seen. I lean over and bring my mouth to hers, swallowing her moans. The kiss is slow and steady. I savor every curve of my tongue around hers.

"You taste so good, Red," Camden murmurs against her clit.

Caressing her tits, I pinch her nipples and tug on them lightly.

She arches her back every time I do it, and Cam only hums approvingly.

He eats her out like a fucking pro, tongue and lips moving with precision, making her writhe. I trail my kisses down her cheek, her jaw, and her neck. Camden slips a finger into her cunt; I close my lips around her nipple. When Yana lets out a needy whimper, Cam adds two more digits. He fucks her with his fingers, his tongue curling and teasing her clit.

Her breathing is so damn shallow. She's close.

I lick and suck the delicate skin of her throat, leaving little marks. I play with her nipples, adding more friction to drive her even higher. Her moans mingle with the wet sound of Camden fingerfucking her, the combination so erotic it brings me dangerously close to coming in my pants.

"*Bozhe, kak horosho...ya seichas...*[1]" She gasps, then falls silent, the intense shudder rolling through her body speaking louder than any words could.

She comes and comes, but Camden doesn't slow until her body goes limp. Eyes closed, she relaxes her legs and presses a hand to her heaving chest.

Camden, smug asshole that he is, breaks into a devilish grin as he gets to his feet. Dropping onto the mattress on her other side, he wipes her arousal off his face, then licks it off his fingers, one by one.

"Isn't she the most delicious thing you've ever tasted?" I ask, my cock so hard it aches.

He smirks. "She is."

"Queen?" I brush my fingers over her cheek, and she opens her eyes. "You were speaking in Russian again, and we want to know what you're babbling about when you come."

"Then maybe you should learn the language." She smiles lazily as she sits up. "But honestly, when I speak in Russian like that, it's because you make me feel good. If it was something you needed to hear, trust me, I would've shouted it in English."

Camden catches my eye, his smile growing wider. "What do you think, Logan? Wanna make her shout and scream?"

"Fuck yes." I bury my face in her neck, kissing and biting her skin.

Yana laughs, the sound low and warm. "No competition, though. I want both of you."

"You've got yourself a team, baby," I murmur against her throat.

---

1. Oh, God, it feels so good...I'm gonna...

Camden tilts her face up and kisses her fiercely, and she gives as good as she gets. It's fast and rough, their tongues battling for dominance, the moment fueling my own arousal even more. Cam and I couldn't be more different if we tried. I'm a slow and steady kind of guy, while my best friend is fast and chaotic. He's burning from the inside, setting her on fire too, and I'll be the one who makes sure they don't demolish each other.

"Take off your clothes," Yana commands, pushing Camden away.

In a matter of seconds, the two of us stand in front of her fully naked.

She bites her bottom lip, trying to suppress her smile. Her eyes glimmer in the dim light as she slides onto the floor, kneeling in front of us.

"You gonna take your sweet time, eh?" Cam taunts her, locking his hands behind his back.

"You're only showing how impatient you are," I comment. I can't miss the opportunity to mess with him, at least a little.

Yana tuts. "Teamwork, guys."

Cam opens his mouth, probably to argue. But then she grips both of our shafts, and as a thrill shoots down my spine, the only noise Camden makes is a low groan. She pumps us both with a deliberate slowness. Once, then twice. The third time, she squeezes the tip of my cock, hard.

"Fuck..." Breathing heavily, I close my eyes, stars bursting behind my lids. "Do it again."

"Only because you asked so nicely," she murmurs. The vixen doesn't disappoint. She repeats the motion over and over, making my legs shake.

It feels so fucking good. In seconds, I lose myself to the fire surging through my veins. I move my hips to the rhythm she's set, staving off an orgasm, but when she takes my cock into her mouth, I know I'm a goner.

"Holy fuck. So warm, so wet," I grumble, peering down at her.

Yana works me over with her mouth while pumping Camden's cock with her hand.

Given the way his eyebrows are pulled together, I know he's teetering at the edge, trying to control himself too.

She pops off my dick and flicks her tongue over the crown while she roughly cups my balls.

Damn. I think I've gone to heaven. There's no way this is real.

She continues sucking me off while jerking Camden. Her enthusiasm is a fucking dream. Our growls and grunts mix with the moans that slip from her.

"Red, I'm so fucking close..." Cam groans, thrusting into her hand.

I grunt. "Me too..."

With a satisfied smile, she moves back and looks up at us. "Tits or face?"

Wow.

I eye Camden, who's fucking grinning. "Tits?"

He dips his chin sharply. "This time."

Stepping closer, I take hold of my dick. Cam takes hold of his, and Yana sits on the floor, sticking out her chest and cupping her breasts. I zero in on her perky nipples, losing myself in the moment. When my release finally hits, I spill myself on her tits with a guttural groan. Cam comes a second later, grunting hard and loud. Then he steps closer and drags his cock around her nipple, painting her chest with our combined release and drawing a moan out of her.

"Ready for round two?" he asks with an arched brow.

She sits back on her heels. "Yes, but I need to clean up first."

We each hold out a hand and help her to her feet, but when she's standing at full height, I steal her away and press a kiss to her lips.

Once she's slipped into the bathroom, Cam and I slump onto the bed. The silence between us doesn't feel heavy or awkward. In fact, it's comfortable. It's like the unspoken understanding we've always had has only gotten stronger.

"I'm glad you're here with us," I tell him.

His lips twitch with the hint of a smile. "I'm glad you talked me into coming."

"Aww, look at you two." Yana strolls into the room, hips swaying.

She's so fucking perfect, and I can't help but stare. "Bonding and opening up. Think you'll want to be each other's boyfriends too?"

Cam narrows his eyes, a mischievous smirk tipping his lips. "Sorry to disappoint, Red." He grabs her wrist and pulls her onto his lap so she's straddling him. "I love my best friend, but I don't swing that way, no matter how close we end up physically while we're fucking you."

"Same for me." I push her wild locks off her face. "We're *your* boyfriends only."

"Okay, okay." Her breath hitches as Camden slides inside her. "More love for me."

"Only for you," he murmurs as she grips his shoulders and rides him.

I cup the back of her neck and tip her head back, licking into her mouth. She moans, sliding her fingers into my hair and tugging.

I pull back, pumping my cock, and take her in. She's a mess. The most stunning mess I've ever seen. Her hair falls over her shoulders, her eyes glimmering with fire, her lips swollen and puffy.

"Let's get more comfortable." Camden stands, guiding Yana's legs around his hips, and positions himself against the headboard. Then he eyes me over her shoulder. "Come here, Logan."

I climb onto the bed, staying on my feet, and stand at her side while she rides his cock and he palms her tits. Without slowing, she twists my way and grabs my dick, urging me to move closer. Then she's taking me into her mouth again.

"Fuck." I grunt, shutting my eyes.

We fall into a rhythm. The room fills with our moans, whimpers, and groans echoing around us. Their bodies slap together, mixing with the sound of her gagging on my cock. I fuck her mouth, enjoying the way she swirls her tongue around its head and how she grazes her teeth around my shaft from time to time while she rotates her hips, fucking Cam hard.

My orgasm is explosive, taking me by surprise as I coat her throat with my cum. She swallows, her watery eyes wide and locked on mine, then quickly falls apart. With a curse, Cam fucks up into her, spilling inside her too.

She falls back, and we join her, flanking her on the mattress, all three of us out of breath. Bodies glistening with sweat, we touch her, tease her, finding ways to make her beg for more with just our fingers.

Like this, her nerve endings alight and overstimulated, every touch brings her close to the edge.

"You sound so fucking sweet," Camden says, voice rough. "Makes me think you're ready for round three."

By some miracle, I'm hard again. Forget needing a comedown period. "I fucking am." I prop myself on my elbow, looking down at Yana. "Wanna get on all fours for me?"

"Why, yes." With a wicked smile, she flips over, her ass in the air. "Get your cock inside me."

Heart still thundering, I situate myself between her legs and place my hands on the small of her back. She arches more, begging to be stuffed, so I give her what she wants, guiding my cock to her entrance and burying myself inside her in one hard thrust. When my vision goes hazy, I hold still and find my bearings. From there, I keep my movements slow and gentle, making sure neither of us comes too soon.

Still lying on his back, Camden presses his fingers to her mouth, tracing her bottom lip, his blue eyes practically glowing with lust.

"I want your cock in my mouth," she tells him breathlessly.

He slips off the bed and stands at the edge near her head. "Open up."

Eagerly, she does what she's told.

"Good girl," I praise her as I slide out until only my tip is still inside her. Then I fuck her in earnest.

Across from me, Camden fucks her throat, and when he catches me looking at him, he breaks into a grin. I can't help but wear a matching expression. Clearly, we're still trying to understand how we got so fucking lucky.

What we're doing doesn't feel like chaos. It doesn't feel wrong.

It's a choice.
Our choice.
And I wouldn't have it any other way.

19
19
Silka.art

## THIRTEEN

# I'm Kind of Dating Them Both

YANA

SOFT MORNING LIGHT FILTERS IN THROUGH THE CABIN window. For the first time in days, there's no raging wind rattling the windows. It's as if the storm has finally moved on. I should be sleeping, but I can't. Not with Logan's hand resting on my hip and Camden's front tucked so tightly against my back. I'm sore after last night, but in a satisfying kind of way. I have zero regrets—only a strong desire to do it again.

If only we could stay here, in this little paradise, longer.

The roads should be cleared by now, and we all have to get back to reality, to practices, matches, games, and airports.

But as much as I want to stay tucked away like this, leaving here doesn't feel like an ending. More like an ellipsis. That promise of "to be continued."

I am theirs, just like they are mine. We established that yesterday. And I'm not letting them go.

Logan mumbles incoherently, his eyes still closed. I cup his cheek, brushing my thumb over his stubble, and he breaks into a beautiful smile.

"Morning," he whispers as he cracks one eye open.

"Good morning." I lean in and press my lips to his. "How did you sleep?"

"It was the best sleep of my life." He winks, then goes rigid, stretching his body out along the mattress. "Though that's not a surprise after the best night of my life."

"You're so cheesy."

"And way too cheerful," Camden grunts with a kiss on my shoulder.

I shift onto my back, and they both instantly tower over me, propping their heads on their knuckles. Logan smiles affectionately, while Camden is wearing a scowl. His eyes are sleepy and his hair is a mess, but when he flicks my nipple and his lips twitch slightly, I know he's more awake than he's letting on.

Logan smooths the wrinkle between my eyebrows with this thumb. "What are you thinking about?"

"Us. This." I survey them both. Bitterness fills my mouth, but I shove it down. "We're leaving today. You have games this week, and I'm leaving for Australia a few days after New Year's. How are we going to make it work?"

"Effortlessly." Camden plants another kiss to my forehead.

Logan caresses my cheek with his fingertips. "This may be the end of our time here, but it's the beginning of so much more."

Camden finally breaks into a real smile. "You're ours now, Red. We're not that easy to chase away."

"And we never shy away from a challenge," Logan says.

I huff. I thought we decided there was no competition.

As if he can read my mind, Logan laughs. "Not between us, Queen. Will our busy schedules make it difficult to find time to see each other? Sure. But we'll make it work. You're worth it."

My heart flutters, like butterflies taking flight. I've never been happier or more at ease. Camden and Logan stir the primal, illogical tendencies inside me while also making me feel like I belong. Like I've finally found my people.

I put my hand on the back of Logan's head and pull him down for a kiss. It's slow and gentle, causing warmth to spread through my body. When he leans away, he's grinning from ear to ear.

Then, without words, he stands, letting Camden take his place.

This kiss is different, fierier and faster. It's exactly what makes these men perfect for me. One is steady, balancing me and making me feel safe and grounded. The other is pure fire, making me reckless and adventurous. With them by my side, I will be unstoppable.

Logan slips into his sweatpants, then tilts his head, surveying us. "What do you think about coming to our next game? You could see us play and spend a little more time with us before you leave for Australia. So we can celebrate this"—he holds up a finger and waves it around, gesturing to the three of us—"properly."

"Yeah," Camden says in my ear, sending a delicious thrill down my spine. "Come to our game, Red. Be there for your boyfriends."

Chuckling, I bury my head in the crook of Camden's neck. "I'll be there."

There's nothing I wouldn't do for these two.

THE ARENA IS ELECTRIC, the crowd roaring, sending energy buzzing through my veins. I've been to plenty of hockey games in Minsk. I've even been to a few Thunders games with Roman's wife. But none of them come close in comparison to this experience.

Watching the guys on the ice does weird things to my body. Excitement mixes with arousal, and beneath that there's a steady sense of pride that these two men are mine. Who knew being with them would turn me into an obsessed, possessive girlfriend?

As far as the public knows, I'm Logan Reid's girlfriend. A famous tennis player dating the Thunders' left winger. That alone caused ruckus on social media. There's no way we could have told the whole story. Not yet, at least, and Camden is okay with that.

When Logan scores, I cheer until my throat's sore. I clap and jump with the rest of the crowd. My chest swells with pride and love. Chloe was supposed to join me, but she got a call from her boss at the last minute. So I came alone, but it doesn't bother me one bit.

Camden is an incredible goalie. He's quick and calm under pressure, his reflexes precise. There's not a trace of his impulsiveness or his explosive persona when he's on the ice.

Once the game is over but before the team has left the ice, I slip away, getting ahead of the crowd so I can congratulate the guys. I show my pass to the security guard, and he lets me into the tunnel, explaining where the family room is. I take note, planning to end up there so I can catch up with Nevaeh, but not yet. First, I want to see my men.

Camden appears in the tunnel first, helmet off, his hair soaked, sweat dripping down his temples. When he spots me, he breaks into a smirk, his eyes flashing.

"Your boyfriend is talking to the press," he drawls.

Okay, maybe he isn't completely at peace with the story we've given the public. But what other option did we have? Announcing our nontraditional relationship would generate the wrong kind of buzz before my season kicks off, and it's not what they need during their regular season either.

With a glance over his shoulder, and then over mine, I step in close. His blue eyes widen, his pupils dilating.

I grab his jersey and pull him into a quick kiss, eager to show him that I'm just as much his as I am Logan's.

His shock only lasts a second. Then he's kissing me back, hard and hungry, like he's been starving for it.

With his forehead pressed to mine, he exhales loudly. "Sorry if I sounded condescending."

"No worries. I know you're a hothead." I beam, stepping back. "But you matter to me. Don't forget that."

"I won't." He gives me a smile.

Logan appears then, grinning, his hair still damp. He pulls me into him and kisses me until I'm out of breath.

"What did you think?" he asks, still holding me close.

"I loved it," I gush. "You were both incredible."

"I knew you'd be a fan."

Camden quirks a brow. "Are you going to watch tomorrow's game? We'll be in Vegas."

"I will. I promise." Then I clear my throat. "I actually have a surprise for you."

"Yeah?" Logan looks down at me.

I grin, my pulse racing. "What do you think about celebrating the new year together, just the three of us?"

Camden breaks into a rare smile. "Hell yeah. Let's do it at my place."

"Deal," Logan and I say at the same time. We eye each other, then break into laughter.

As they disappear into the locker room, I notice Roman standing a few feet away, helmet in hand, giving me a puzzled look.

I wave at him. "*Privet. Kak dela?*[1]"

"*Privet*[2]." He stops in front of me, a deep wrinkle between his eyebrows. "*Ya zadam tebe odin vopros, i budet kruto esli ty otvetish chestno, potomu chto mne kazhetsya ya udarilsya golovoy slishkom sil'no vo vremya igry.*[3]"

I frown at his cryptic wording, but I nod.

"Are you and Logan together?"

"Yes."

"*Aga*[4]." He threads his fingers through his blond hair. "Please don't be mad when I ask you my next question, okay?"

"Okay, *no ty menya pugaesh*[5]."

He snorts, shaking his head. "*Kto by govoril*[6]." He swallows thickly and scans our surroundings. "I saw you and Camden kissing, and I'm certain Logan did too. But then the three of you were talking as if nothing happened, and you even kissed Logan once he joined you. What is that about?"

---

1. Hi. How are you?
2. Hi
3. I'm gonna ask you something, and it will be awesome if you can answer honestly, because I really think I hit my head too hard during the game
4. Uh-huh
5. but you're scaring me
6. Look who's talking

Cheeks flaming, I lower my gaze to my feet. Shit. I'm nowhere near prepared to explain our situation.

"Yana?"

With a defeated sigh, I look him in the eye. "I'm kind of dating them both."

Roman stares at me, his expression unreadable. "I'm too old for this."

"Roma!" I smack his shoulder.

He erupts into laughter that echoes off the cement walls. "Whatever floats your boat, I guess." He winks. "*Prosto bud' schastliva.Vsye ostal'noe nevazhno.*[7]"

"Thank you." I lean in and give him a quick hug. "Don't tell anyone. Please."

"Of course." He breaks into a devilish grin. "But there's no way I'm keeping this from Nev."

I grasp his arm. "Please, let me tell her, okay? Is she in the family room?"

"She's at home. She had a busy day at work, so she promised to watch from the living room." With a wink, he skirts around me, heading for the locker room. "Don't worry, I won't say anything to your *boyfriends*...for now."

Fuck. With any luck, the guys will be too excited about my surprise to worry about Roman.

---

7. Just be happy. Everything else doesn't matter

## FOURTEEN

# Midnight Kisses

### CAMDEN

LOGAN'S SPRAWLED OUT ON THE COUCH IN MY LIVING room, scrolling on his phone. A soccer game is playing on TV, the volume low. He's in a white shirt and dark blue jeans, and his hair is a perfect mess, as usual.

He couldn't care less that his shirt will be wrinkled by the time Yana gets here. Honestly, I kind of admire his nonchalance.

Me? I'm full of pent-up excitement. Energy bubbles inside me, pushing me to pace back and forth while we wait. Not only am I still keyed up after the game, but I'm anxious about having Yana here for the first time.

It'll probably be the last too, at least for a while, since she's leaving for Australia in a couple of days. Dammit. For someone who's never really been in a steady relationship, I sure got attached to this girl fast.

"You're gonna wear a hole in the carpet," Logan mutters without looking up.

"Shut up," I shoot back. "I just can't wait for her to be here. She's been secretive the past few days, don't you think? What if she doesn't show?"

He smirks and finally meets my eye. "She'll be here. This is Yana we're talking about. She's full of motivation and determination. If she said she'd be here, then she will be."

I grunt, but my chest tightens anyway. He's right, and it annoys the hell out of me. We're supposed to be equals in this relationship, but he's her official boyfriend, while I'm just her boyfriend's best friend, a teammate.

Fuck, I'm falling down the rabbit hole again.

Yana is ours. Not his, not mine. *Ours*. I need to focus on that.

The doorbell rings, startling me, and with a glance at Logan, I hurry to the hallway. Already, my heart thrashes against my ribs. A month ago, if someone had told me I'd be this nervous about a girl, I would've thought they'd lost their mind. Yet here I am. The emotions she brings out in me are nothing like anything I've experienced before. Every sensation—happiness, passion, and the desire to possess her—is strong.

When I open the door, my jaw hits the floor. Yana is wearing a leather jacket and a shimmering dark green dress that looks like it was made from pure sin. The skirt is short, causing my pulse to spike and making her legs look impossibly long.

Logan joins me in the doorway, his shoulder brushing mine, and whistles low. "Wow, you look like a real queen."

"Holy shit," I mutter. "You're fucking divine."

Beaming, she steps inside. "Happy Almost-New Year."

THE NIGHT BLURS, full of laughter, conversations about our game, about the Thunders' season, and her training. Champagne flows, and music echoes off the walls.

The dinner Logan and I made was a success. Yana moaned more than once while we ate, tempting me to lay her out on the table and have my way with her right then. But by some miracle, I resisted.

After dinner, we turn on *Love Actually*, though we don't really watch it. Yana rests against my chest, and I splay a hand over her collarbone. Her feet are in Logan's lap, and he's lightly dragging his fingertips over her ankle.

"Were your parents okay with you not flying to DC for New Year's?" Yana asks Logan.

"Yeah." He dips his chin. "And I warned them that I won't have time to visit until February."

I put my mouth to her ear. "What about you, huh? Why didn't you fly home?"

"I thought about it, but before Christmas, my mood was all over the place. I didn't think it was a good idea to actually go home." She sighs. "I've been in a funk since my ex cheated on me. Then, the end of my season was a disaster. Facing them after all that...it was just too much. My family can read me like an open book. I didn't want them to see what a mess I was."

I blink, my heart skipping a beat. There's no way she said what I think she said.

"Excuse me." Frowning, Logan tilts forward. "Did you just say that your ex cheated on you?"

She chuckles, the sound humorless. "I guess I did. He cheated on me in my apartment. I caught them in my bed."

Blood boiling, I clench my jaw. "I'd love to have a chat with him."

Logan locks eyes with me. "Me too."

Her silvery laughter breaks the tension that's suddenly shrouded us. "I'm flattered that you'd stand up for me like that, but he's not worth it. I was ashamed at first. Embarrassed that it happened to me. That I didn't notice the signs, ignored some real red flags. At the end of the day, he showed his true colors, and I had the strength to walk away. But the breakup took a toll on me mentally, and I missed the WTA Finals. I'm grateful for it all now. If not for the state I was in, I would've gone home for the holidays, and then I wouldn't have met you two."

"When you put it like that...I guess I'm glad he cheated on you," I say gruffly.

Logan barks out a laugh, shaking his head. "What I think Cam meant to say is that we're sorry you had to go through that. You are fucking magic, and you didn't deserve it, but it's that asshole's loss.

He didn't cherish you or appreciate what he had, and now you're with us. And we'll never treat you like that."

My cheeks burn. Dammit. I truly should've watched my mouth. "Yeah, sorry. We would never hurt you, Yana. That's a promise."

"Thank you," she murmurs, snuggling into me. "And while you're in such a good mood, I need to talk about something that might upset you."

My body stiffens. It's a natural reaction to bad news, but I can't speak.

"Um," she says, her eyes downcast, "Roman knows."

Logan quirks a brow. "Knows what?"

"About us. That I'm dating both of you."

"What?" I heave out a breath. "How did he—"

"He saw me kissing you, and then he saw me kissing Logan—and he saw the three of us talking afterward like it wasn't a big deal."

"How did you find out he knows? Did he just ask you outright?" Logan asks, his brows pulled together.

"Yeah, but that's how he and I are. Straightforward. It's probably related to our cultural background. He was being kinda nosy, but we're good friends, so I can't be mad." She shrugs. "And he promised not to say anything to anyone."

Chewing on the inside of my cheek, I assess Logan. "Now I understand why he was staring at us that day in the locker room."

"He probably thinks we're crazy," Logan muses, threading his fingers through his hair.

Rather than be upset, I can't help but be grateful for what we have. "Or that we're lucky to have a girl like Yana."

The alarm I set so we wouldn't miss the ball drop goes off. Once I've silenced it, I grab the remote and switch to the live stream in Times Square.

"The countdown, huh?" Yana leans away to look at me.

I grin. "I've always loved the tradition of kissing someone at midnight."

"Kissing the girl he's head over heels for can make a guy's whole year." Logan moves closer.

Smiling, Yana sits up between us. Logan takes her hand in his as I snake my arm around her waist.

"Three," I say.

"Two," Logan continues, along with the host.

"One," Yana whispers.

She kisses Logan first, soft and sweet like it always is. Then she turns to me and kisses me like she means to set me on fire.

And she does. I'm ablaze, full of need. So I scoop her into my arms and carry her straight to my bedroom on the second floor.

Logan shuts the door behind us as I set her on her feet and take a step back. With her between us like this, it's like we're circling her, hunting her.

Logan unzips her dress, and I help her pull it over her head. While he unclasps her bra and tosses it on the floor, I push her panties down. She laughs breathlessly as I crouch in front of her so she can step out of them.

"Two against one." She clutches my shirt and tugs me closer. "It's not fair."

"It's all about teamwork." Logan loops an arm around her waist from behind and kisses her shoulder.

"And about doing everything we can for you," I tell her, holding her gaze as she unbuttons my shirt.

In response to that comment, a devilish glint flares in her eyes, and she takes a step back from me.

I arch an eyebrow and reach for her.

"If you're set on doing everything you can for me..." She skirts around me, moving so that she steps out of Logan's hold too. "How about you strip for me? Both of you."

She lowers herself onto the bed and rests back on her hands. The sight of her makes my mouth water. Her body is perfect, her beauty effortless. Her copper-red hair is like a curtain over her shoulders, framing her face and accentuating her porcelain skin. Every inch of her was created to be admired. Admired by us.

Logan strips out of his shirt, then works his belt loose. It takes me a second to come back to reality, but I'm right behind him, quickly shucking off my clothes.

When we're standing in front of her fully naked, a sinful smile spreads across her face. "*Kakie horoshie mal'chiki*[1]," she murmurs, beckoning us closer with her finger. "I have a surprise for you."

"Whatever it is, it couldn't be better than you. Than this," Logan says, his eyes not leaving her body.

"I don't know..." she teases. "I might just prove you wrong."

I sit on one side of her while Logan settles on the other. With her sandwiched between us, the heat of her body soaks into me, setting my skin aflame. She wraps her hands around our dicks, slowly jerking them, already making my vision darken.

I brace myself on my hands behind me and close my eyes. *Fuck yes.*

"I want to try something new," she whispers.

My eyes snap open, and when I look at her, Logan is watching too.

"What is it?" he asks.

"I've never done it before." Her smirk damn near kills me. "I want both of you inside me. At the same time."

I swear I black out for a second. It's not what I expected to hear, but I'm all in. Warmth infuses my body, my chest expanding.

"Are you sure?" Logan cups her cheek, urging her to look at him.

"I am." She presses her lips to his. Then she rears back, and on an exhale, she says, "I came prepared."

I lick my dry lips. "Prepared?"

Her grin widens as she turns to me. "I'm wearing a plug."

For a second, the world tilts. Heat punches straight through me, sharp and raw.

Logan swears under his breath, shaking his head like he can't believe it.

"You're fucking insane," I rasp, but I'm grinning.

"Or brilliant," she bites back, wiggling her eyebrows.

"You totally are," I agree. "Never fucking doubt it, Red."

---

1. Such good boys

Logan helps her move to the middle of my bed, peppering her lips and neck with light kisses while I round the mattress and climb on from the other side, hovering over them. He positions himself between her legs and licks her pussy, sucking and teasing her clit with his tongue. I can't help but watch her, drink in her every reaction. She's so fucking stunning. It's a crime to be so irresistible.

"Camden..." My name on her lips sends a shiver down my spine. "I want your cock...in my mouth."

Heart pounding, I sweep her hair away from her face. "I'd never say no to you."

She lets out a laugh that quickly turns into a moan as Logan doubles his efforts.

I move closer, and when she closes her lips around my dick, I throw my head back and groan. It's everything.

With my cock in her mouth, she cups my balls, massaging and then tugging on them. I lick my fingers and play with her nipples, adding to the intensity of what Logan is doing. The sound he makes as he devours her mixed with the way she gags on my cock only heightens my pleasure. I've never had such an incredible blow job. She's acing it, just like everything else in her life.

Before long, she moves her hips up and down, matching the speed with which Logan strokes her inner walls with his fingers, her sounds becoming more desperate. She sucks harder on the head of my cock and then releases it with a pop, again and again and again, until I come inside her mouth. She swallows my release, then grins up at me.

I shift back and kiss her, plundering her mouth with my tongue. Tasting myself only pushes me to ravish her more, kiss her so hard she's gasping for air. Her back arches then, and she cries out, clamping her legs together. Logan doesn't stop devouring her as he pushes her knees apart again, helping her to prolong her orgasm.

"You're my most favorite dessert." He sits up, wiping her arousal from his face, wearing a smug expression.

Yana props herself on her elbows, her eyes heavy-lidded, her chest still rising and falling rapidly. "I want both of you inside me. Now."

"I love it when you're bossy." Logan winks at her, then meets my gaze. "What do you think?"

I nod at the pillows. "Lie down so she can straddle you."

"Now you're talking." Quickly, he obeys.

It takes everything in me not to tell him that he's "such a good boy," mostly to taunt him, but also because I'm impressed with how eager he is.

Yana mounts him, and he guides his dick to her entrance and eases her lower. When he's buried to the hilt, he puts his hand on the back of her neck and pulls her down for a kiss. She rides him slowly, the two of them moving like they've coordinated each detail. It's fucking beautiful. Once I've found the strength to look away, I get on my knees behind her and put my hand on her back, pushing her against Logan's chest.

The sight of the plug in her ass makes my dick instantly hard, even though I just came minutes ago.

I pull it out slowly, stopping before the tip pops out, then push it back in. She moans loudly, and Logan covers her mouth with his, muffling her sounds. I repeat the motion over and over, loosening the tight ring of muscle and getting her body ready.

She lifts her head and glances at me over her shoulder. "There's a bottle of lube in my purse."

A thrill shoots down my spine, and I back away. "You planned everything, didn't you?"

In less than a minute, I've retrieved the lube from her purse downstairs and am positioned behind her again, pulling the plug in and out, using it to drive her wild.

When she's languid, I squirt a generous amount of lube on my cock and then ease the plug out.

A shuddering moan escapes her lips at the loss.

"Red," I soothe, using my lubed-up fingers to stretch her further, "I need you to relax. I'll go slow, and if something doesn't feel right, tell me," I say as I line up my cock with her entrance.

"If it's too much, tell us," Logan adds, his hands on her ass, spreading her open for me.

"Okay," she whispers. "I'm ready."

Despite the fire surging in my veins, tempting me to slam into her, I push my crown into her slowly. "Is that okay?"

"Yeah..." she pants. "Keep going..."

Inch by inch, I slip inside her, moving past the ring of muscle, then pulling out. Again and again, I repeat the movement, going deeper each time, until I'm fully seated.

"You're taking us so well, baby," Logan murmurs as he pushes her hair off her face.

With calculated slowness, I pull back and slide inside her ass a little faster, only stopping when my balls make contact with her skin. It's so tight and so fucking good, it takes everything in me not to come on the spot.

"Fuck," I groan, jaw clenched and muscles tight.

With my hands on her waist, I move, fucking her from behind.

In minutes, her loud moans echo off the ceiling. Logan groans and whimpers, caressing her face. His tenderness balances my rough edges, the best of both worlds for our girl.

"It feels so good," she murmurs. "I'm gonna come so hard...More, please..."

"Greedy girl," I growl as my release barrels down on me.

"More," she begs.

"Such a good girl," Logan whispers against her lips. "Taking both our cocks...like the Queen you are."

I fuck her faster, my eyes squeezed shut to stave off my orgasm.

"Fuck, Cam, she's fucking strangling me..." Logan mutters. "Shit..." He lets out a guttural noise and goes rigid beneath her.

With both of our names spilling from her lips, she falls apart, coming hard and wild, thrashing between us. Her reaction triggers my release, and I spill inside her too, feeling more powerful than ever.

Once I ease out of her, I slump onto my back, and Logan and I shift, making room for Yana between us. Her chest rises and falls quickly, her hair in total disarray against my pillows. She's still trembling from the intensity of her orgasm, but the smile on her face is immaculate.

I swear I've never seen anything so beautiful.

# Epilogue

YANA

***Seven months later***

THE CROWD IS LOUD, A CACOPHONY OF CHEERS AND applause, but my world has narrowed to the grass beneath my feet, the racket in my hand, and the neon green ball. My arm burns, and sweat stings my eyes, but I push away the sensations. Point after point, game after game, I stay locked in.

Since the Australian Open at the start of the season, I've played better and better. My stats have never been this good. I've fought for every point, working hard to prove—mostly to myself—that last year's slip was a one-time thing. That I can play at the championship level. After the semifinals in Melbourne, I won in Madrid and Rome, then finished with a quarterfinal in Paris. That's progress I'm beyond proud of. I started at number eight in the WTA rankings, and now I'm sitting at number six.

I bounce the ball three times, my hand steady even though my pulse is racing. Match point. One more serve, and I'll close this out. I breathe in, then toss the ball high, exhale, and drive it down the T with everything I have left.

Müller stretches for it but barely clips the frame, and the return flies long. For a moment, I stand frozen in place as the roar of Centre Court crashes over me.

I've earned my spot in the Wimbledon semifinals.

*Bozhe moyi. Ya v polufinale*[1]!

I smile, taking in the thunderous crowd, searching for my men. When I find them, my heart flips. Logan stands tall in the stands, clapping like his life depends on it, his grin brighter than the sun. Beside him, Camden stands with his arms crossed. His expression is sharp, but his eyes are locked on mine, burning with desire. For half a heartbeat, the noise falls away, the fans disappear, and it's just us—me and these two gorgeous men. *My* gorgeous men.

Camden mouths, "Focus," snapping me out of my reverie. With a shake of my head, I turn my attention to the crowd and wave. Their support has been phenomenal, and I couldn't be more grateful for their encouragement.

After one more wave, I head to the net and give Elke a quick hug. "You were amazing," I tell her.

She smiles, her eyes watery. "But not as amazing as you."

"Maybe next time."

"Really looking forward to it," she says as we both stride to the chair umpire to shake hands.

The next thirty minutes are a whirlwind. When I find myself in front of the press, I'm hit with question after question about the match, about the tournament, about my opponent. Then comes a question I've had to answer many times since Australia.

"How much of this success do you credit to your boyfriend, Logan Reid?" an American journalist asks.

I keep my smile in place, but it tightens. "Logan is incredibly supportive of me and my career, just like I am of him," I say calmly. "But when I'm on the court, it's just me, my racket, and the ball. No one else can score points for me."

A few chuckles ripple through the room, and a pang pierces my chest. Why does it always take this turn? I had a successful career

1. Oh my God. I'm in the semifinals!

before I met Logan, but suddenly, the world thinks I'm only winning because of him? As if without a man in my life I'm not worthy of such accomplishments?

Ironically, the press never asks Logan whether he thinks our relationship is the reason he had his best season yet.

Another reporter chimes in, studying me with a tilt of his head. "Still, your boyfriend had an amazing season. The Thunders lost in the finals, just one step from lifting the Cup. I can't imagine having him here doesn't help. Do you think you play better when he's watching?"

I let out a slow breath, balling my fists, and keep my tone even. "I think I play better when I remember who I am and what I'm capable of. When I trust *myself*." I pause, relax my hands, and put my palms flat on the table in front of me. "I'm happy when my boyfriend has a chance to see me play in person. It's great to have his support, but that support doesn't go away when he's not here. He watches my matches on TV when his team is traveling, and I do the same for him. Our relationship is a partnership, based on love and respect. Logan knows I appreciate his support and how much it means to me. I don't need an interview to prove it to him."

That shuts them up, at least for today.

By the time I head down the hallway of the hotel, my jaw aches from forcing so many smiles. All I need is them.

Only being in the presence of Logan and Camden can help me.

When I push open the door of my room, soft music reaches my ears. Familiar music. Lips twisted into a smile, I shuffle to the living area, where Logan and Camden are sprawled out on the couch. *The Lord of the Rings* is playing on the TV, and the two of them are focused on the screen.

I tiptoe closer and wrap my arms around Logan's shoulders. "I missed you," I murmur in his ear.

"Goddammit!" Camden yelps, bolting upright. "When did you get here?"

Laughing, Logan pulls me over the back of the couch and into his lap. He holds me close, the warmth of his naked chest slipping under my skin. "How was the press conference?"

"You don't wanna know," I mutter, cuddling into him. "While most of the journalists are great, there are always a few who think I'm only playing this well because you're my boyfriend."

Camden snorts. "What, they think he dicks you down so well that it leads you to victory?"

So many things have changed since we decided to be together after our snowed-in Christmas. My family knows about our relationship. Logan's too. They don't always understand, but they are supportive, and they all love Cam. Because what's not to love? Especially when he puts his guard down and lets everyone see the real him—a kind and caring guy who wants the best for his closest people. My best friends Karina and Chloe know too, and the latter keeps saying I'm living her dream. The guys from the Thunders know, and with how close they are—there's zero judgment. As for everyone else? We don't care. We're happy and in love, and that's the only thing that matters.

And even though Logan is my official boyfriend, Camden owns me just as much as he does, and he's fine with it. Though he keeps insisting that if we ever decide to have a baby, the first one should be his. But...that's not in our plans. At least for a while.

"I guess. Or maybe that winning is contagious. That I caught it from him."

Camden breaks into a wicked smile. "Little do they know that you have two hockey players fucking you so hard that some days you can't even walk straight."

I kick at him, but he catches my foot and holds it in his lap. When he massages my heel, I moan and melt into Logan.

"In all seriousness, don't pay attention to those assholes," Logan says softly. "They're idiots if they can't comprehend the idea of a woman earning success without the help of a man. You were phenomenal on the court today, and you deserve that win more than anyone."

"That last match point left me speechless." Camden adds more pressure as he continues working his magic on my foot. "And you know that doesn't happen often."

"Thank you so much. Both of you." I smile at Camden and then look over my shoulder at Logan. "You're my lifesavers."

I settle in for the second half of the movie, lounging in Logan's arms, my hand in Camden's. Occasionally, Logan presses his lips to the top of my hair, whispering about how proud of me he is. And just as often, Camden flashes me a smile, his eyes softening in a way they only do for me.

Later, in bed between them, I can't help but think about the dinner where I met them. About the cabin in the woods where we were forced together.

Being snowed in like that was like a match point. We aced it, using the time to our advantage. And we won the greatest prize of all.

Us.

If I had the chance to do it all over again, I wouldn't change a thing.

# Bonus Chapter 1

## LOGAN

***Three years later***

Shoulder propped against the doorframe, I stand and watch the guests dance. We didn't want to have too many people and still ended up with almost eighty. My family, Yana's family, our friends, my teammates and their wives and kids. It should be crowded and too loud, but I think it's just right. Everyone came here to celebrate our wedding, and they are here to support us on this new journey.

If someone told me that I'd get together with the love of my life after spending only four days stranded in a cabin during the storm, I wouldn't believe them. Because before Yana I thought that for the relationship to be strong, you need to get to know the person you're getting together with in and out. Like you need to see them in good and in bad, you need to learn about their past and their plans for the future. Surely, we talked about some of it, but it wasn't that deep. And yet, after just four days together with her and Camden—I knew she was the one.

And every day since I've been falling for her more and more.

I find her on the dance floor and drink her in. Hair collected in a neat bun, not a lock out of place. Minimal makeup that I knew took some time to make, highlighting her beautiful eyes in the most exquisite way. The dress, though? I'm speechless. It moves along with her like it was made out of light. From the front, it's simple—clean lines, smooth fabric falling in a long, elegant sweep behind her. The cap sleeves shimmer every time she turns, tiny beads catching the soft lights like they're winking at me.

But it's the back that kills me.

When she spins, the open back flashes into view. This deep, breathtaking V edged with delicate lace that looks like it was stitched right onto her skin. The detail is unreal, all soft floral patterns tracing her spine, disappearing into the curve of her waist. And the row of little white buttons at the bottom...damn. She looks ethereal. Like she stepped out of some dream I've been having my whole life without knowing it.

A bright smile lights up her face as she twirls my sister, making the latter laugh. Lucy is eleven, and she absolutely adores my wife. I kid you not, whenever we visit my parents, Yana is the one Lucy wants to spend her time with, not me. Though I'm not complaining. I'm happy and grateful that my family accepted the woman I love as their own and that they accepted our nontraditional relationship too. This one was probably the hardest, but after three years together, I think everyone who had doubts, now knows that we make it work.

Because being in a relationship with Yana, while she's also in a relationship with Camden, is the only way I know. The only way I want it to be. They are my everything.

"There you are." Camden ambles closer and stops in front of me. He holds out a glass of whiskey to me, and I take it. "I thought you'd be dancing."

"Decided to step away and just watch the crowd." I take a sip of my drink. "Having fun?"

He shrugs. "Yeah. Never thought I'd be a fan of weddings, but yours is cool."

"It took way too much time for us to plan everything for you to say you don't like it."

"I said it's cool." He smirks, shifting to stand by my side. His eyes immediately land on Yana with Lucy. "She's stunning. This dress looks like it was made from clouds. Light and pure."

"She is." I smile. "And you're absolutely right about the dress. I just...I had no words when I saw her for the first time today."

"You were also crying."

I chuckle. "Says the guy who almost tripped over his own feet when her dad brought her to me."

"Guilty."

We fall in a comfortable silence, both calm and content. He's been my best friend since forever, and I can honestly say he's never been more at ease than he's been in the past three years. Our friendship grew stronger, and the understanding we share is just out of this world. I often don't even need him to say something to know what he is thinking about. In tune. With each other, and with Yana.

She is our fire, while we are the oxygen and heat. One is out of the equation, and the fire starts to wither. That's why we always try to sneak at least one trip to each other a month. It's harder when she's on the road for her tournaments, flying all over the world from country to country, and we have our regular season. Harder, but not impossible, because she is our motivation. Our guiding force, and I think I love her even more just for that.

Because she gave me the purpose.

"Are you going to join us tonight?" I ask, not taking my eyes off Yana.

"No. It's your night. Your first night as a husband and a wife, and I don't want to ruin it."

I shake my head and turn to look at him. "You never ruin anything. You are part of us. Part of our family."

"I know it, Logan. She's mine, just as much as she's yours. And I'm still staking my claim on the first baby." He flashes an unashamed grin.

Head thrown back, I laugh. We've had this talk several times, and I'm fine with it, just like Yana, but his constant desire to remind me about it is ridiculous. "You sound like Rumpelstiltskin. You know that, right?"

"I don't care. The firstborn will be mine," he says cheerfully. "And I don't think I should join you tonight also because we're hitting the road quite early tomorrow morning, and if I'll be in the bedroom with the two of you—the night will be long."

"You have a point. The cabin is waiting for the three of us."

He shivers. "I only hope at least this time we won't be stuck there like last year we went there for Christmas."

"Dunno. I kinda like the whole 'snowed-in' fantasy."

"I'm sure you do."

The song ends and Lucy runs to our parents, leaving Yana alone. I push myself away from the doorframe and glance at Camden. "I better go join my wife."

He nods, a smile playing on his lips that is open and genuine. "You better do it. Red looks way too gorgeous to dance alone."

I can't even argue with that, but truthfully, she can do whatever the hell she wants. She's a queen. She sets the rules, and I just happily follow.

For her, I will do absolutely anything.

The party has finally begun to settle, the once-packed dance floor thinning until only a few couples sway in the soft glow of the string lights. I barely notice anything else, though, my world shrinking down to one thing only as my eyes are trained on Yana.

*My wife.*

*Yana Lipnitskaja Reid*. I don't know, but to me, it sounds right.

The music changes and "Perfect" by Ed Sheeran starts playing for the third time tonight. A deep chuckle rambles out of my mouth, and I pull her tighter against my chest. Her skin is hot. I can feel it even through the fabric of her dress. Eyes glimmering, she holds my gaze, a beautiful smile on her lips.

"You and your love for this song," I murmur.

"It's not a crime to love a song so much, especially when you fantasized a lot of times on how you would dance to it at your own wedding."

"I remember." I drop my forehead to hers. "God, I can't believe you're my wife now."

"Konechno twoya[1]." She sighs and closes her eyes. "A ty moy muzh.[2]"

"Yeah, only yours," I reply.

I'm happy I decided to study Russian two years ago. I can better understand her now, even though this language is hard as fuck, especially considering how different it is from English. But I'm a determined guy, and I can proudly say that I can even hold a little conversation with Yana's parents now.

We sway to the rhythm, lost in the moment and in each other. It really feels like it's just the two of us. The rest of the world doesn't exist. She shifts and puts her head against my shoulder.

"Are you tired?" I whisper.

"Just a little bit." She lets out a giggle. "But I'm not tired for our wedding night."

"I've been counting on it." I lean away and look her in the eye. "I can't wait to spend eternity with you."

"Me neither." She closes the gap between us and kisses me softly. "Ya lyublyu tebya[3].“

"A ya lyublyu tebya[4]," I say. Then I kiss her again.

Even when the song ends and another one starts, we don't stop. We dance, we smile, we kiss. Because this—the quiet moment on the dance floor with other people surrounding us—is still just ours.

Sometimes love really just sneaks up on you when you least expect it. It's like a little seed that takes a root in your heart after you meet your person, and with each day it grows, it blooms. Bad days happen, we're all human after all, and we all make mistakes. What makes the

1. Of course I'm yours
2. And you're my husband
3. I love you
4. I love you too

difference is our desire to protect our love no matter what, to cultivate it, to make it stronger, more tangible. Until it becomes bigger than you, bigger than the person you love, bigger than life, and that's why it's never-ending.

Yana is the love of my life. I fell in love pretty much at first sight. I still love her, and no matter how many years would pass—I'll love her forever.

# Bonus Chapter 2

## CAMDEN

***Two years later***

I step out of the cabin, the cold air hitting my face in an instant. The snow is everywhere, covering the trees, the mountains in the distance, and especially our cars. Just the view makes me nostalgic. So many memories connected to this place. So many more we're going to create. On days like this, I'm one hundred percent sure that I made the right decision when I bought this cabin as my wedding gift to Yana and Logan two years ago.

It's *our* cabin. The place that started everything for us and made me the happiest. And it's definitely not something I ever expected to happen.

A shiver runs down my spine when a dust of chilly air washes over me, slipping under my hoodie. Right. I need to make a call to Logan. Hopefully, he's still in town and will be able to go to the store before he comes here.

"Hey, man," Logan says after the third ring. "What's up?"

"What time do you think you're going to be at the cabin?"

"Around six, like I said yesterday. Why?"

Five more hours? Damn, I'll need to figure out something to occupy her so she'll forget about the berries she wants.

I rub the back of my neck, suddenly feeling sheepish. "Your wife is being extremely capricious today."

A bolt of his booming laughter makes me pull my phone away from my ear.

"It's not funny," I grumble. "I thought she was going to bite my head off when I told her we didn't bring strawberries with us."

"It *is* funny, Cam. Yana is my wife, but she's *your* pregnant girlfriend." He snorts. "Her being capricious is on you. How could you forget to bring strawberries?" he mocks.

"Har har. We were shopping together, if you forgot, and we had raspberries on the list because that's what she wanted yesterday."

"Yesterday was so long ago." He barely hides his laughter, and instead of it pissing me off as it would've happened before, I find it amusing.

So many things have changed since I've fallen in love with Yana.

"Indeed, it was so long ago." I sigh and prop my shoulder against the porch column. "Sorry, I just panicked...because I hate seeing her sad or angry."

"I bet she's not angry, just a bit in her feels. She loves you, and you're fully capable of making her mood better. I'm sure by the time I'm going to be at the cabin, she will be back to being our beautiful queen."

"She's always our queen. Just right now she's a bit terrifying." I snicker, shaking my head. "Whenever you'll be on your way, can you please stop by the store and buy strawberries? And blueberries, and also bilberries."

"Aye, captain. Will do." The sound of the car starting reaches my ear. "I better go. I still have a few places to visit before I hit the road. See you tonight."

"See you."

I pocket my phone and take a deep breath. The cold air slides down my throat and straight to my lungs, making my chest expand. The air here is always cleaner, more wholesome. It smells like pine and frosty freshness, and a bit of citrus. Despite that there are still three more days, I can almost taste Christmas on the tip of my tongue, and it puts a smile on my face. Before Yana, this time of the year always smelled like cinnamon and apples and my grandma's pierogies. Now it's also full of tangerines, chocolate, and vanilla. And her favorite Napoleon cake...well, to be fair, it's Logan's and my favorite too. Everything about her is perfect for us.

With another deep breath, I turn around and return to the cabin. The Christmas tree with red-and-white Christmas tree balls, tinsel, and Christmas lights stands in the corner, catching my attention effortlessly. There are quite a few gifts that each of us brought for each other, and I'm excited to see Yana's and Logan's reactions to the gifts I bought for them. Sure, getting gifts is nice, but it's so much better to see a look of pure joy on the faces of your closest people when they tear the wrapper and find what you got for them.

I shake off my shoes, and just as I straighten, her arms are around my torso.

"I'm sorry," she murmurs. "I shouldn't have snapped at you. I feel stupid."

A smile breaks over my lips as I slowly turn to look at her. My breath hitches, just like always, whenever I take her in. Her copper-red hair is collected in a messy bun on top of her head, a few wild locks framing her face. The gray-green color of her eyes makes me wish our little girl will follow after her mommy because that's the most captivating eye color I've ever seen. Her dark green tee is long and loose, covering her cotton shorts, and yet her baby bump is perfectly visible. She's five months along, and I swear all these months I've been literally on cloud nine.

Even when the Thunders lose, the sadness and disappointment that usually would've crept in don't feel the same now. All because of her.

"You're not stupid." I take her chin between my thumb and index finger. "You're the most intelligent woman I've ever met."

"Highly doubt it. An intelligent woman wouldn't have thrown a tantrum over the lack of strawberries...strawberries I didn't even want yesterday."

I cover her lips with mine, slow and gentle. She relaxes in my arms, her body growing soft. Then I start peppering her face with my lips, saying between my kisses, "Logan promised to get to the store before he comes here. He'll buy you strawberries, blueberries, and bilberries."

"*Oh bozhe*, you two are the best!" She grabs my hoodie and pulls me toward her, going backward. She glances over her shoulder, then steps back. Lowering herself on the couch, she holds my gaze. The shift in the atmosphere is subtle, but I notice it anyway. I always notice everything about her.

I pull off my hoodie and toss it to the floor. The crackling sound of the fire in the fireplace mixes with another soviet movie she likes to watch before Christmas playing on the screen of a huge TV that we installed last year—*The Irony of Fate*. I actually like this one. It's very Christmasy to me and very symbolic because the irony of fate is the only thing I can use to explain how I ended up in a relationship with Yana.

"What do you want, Red?" I ask her teasingly as I unzip my fly.

"*Tebya*[1]."

"You have me."

She pouts falsely, her eyes full of mischief. "Do I?" She moves to the edge of the couch and sneaks her hand under my tee. "I certainly don't have your cock inside me."

Dammit. There was zero chance of us not fucking at least once before Logan gets here. Not that I'm complaining. I love fucking her. I love watching him fuck her. I love when we fuck her together. The stamina this girl possesses matches Logan and mine in the most astonishing way. Before her pregnancy, when we didn't see each other much because of her schedule and our regular season, whenever we did get back together—we could've spent the whole day in bed. Fucking, talking, making love, laughing, watching movies together, discussing our careers, making plans for vacation, fucking again.

Still, I take a step back, putting a distance between us. Eyebrows pinched together, she studies me as I get rid of my clothes and stand in

1. You

front of her fully naked. She traps her bottom lip between her teeth, her chest rising and falling quicker.

I wrap my hand around my shaft and start jerking myself. Yana's gaze is glued to my dick, following every movement of my hand. I don't rush. Enjoying the fire building inside me, not only because of what I'm doing, but also because she's watching me.

Her attention is something I'll never stop craving. At this point, I'm utterly and completely hooked on Yana. There's no way it would ever change.

"You're strangely quiet, Red," I tease her, squeezing the head of my cock tighter.

"That's because I'm enjoying the view." She lets her gaze move from my face and down my chest and my dick. Then she brings her eyes back to mine, and the glimmer in her eyes is familiar to me. "Though I'm so wet already...and I'm so sensitive. I can come right here right now without you having your way with me."

I smile, knowing that she got me. Teasing her is fun, but I want to come with her warm pussy strangling my dick.

Glancing between the fireplace and the couch, I settle on the first option. With a nod of my head, I gesture for her to join me on the fluffy rug in front of the fireplace. She grins and stands up as I lie down on my back. The heat coming from the fire is nothing in comparison to how hot my skin already is just from her eyes on me.

Yana slowly takes off her tee and then pushes down her shorts. Stunning. Perfect. Immaculate. Her tits are round and full. Her baby bump is very pronounced. I continue moving my hand up and down my shaft, smearing pre-cum all over it. Fuck. She's not the only one who can come right here right now.

"I need you," I say hoarsely.

Her face lights up with a smile as she comes closer, and I help her to lower herself on my lap. Eyes locked on each other, the connection between us only growing deeper. More emotional. She hoists herself up as I align my dick with her pussy. As slowly as possible, she takes my cock inside her. Inch by inch until I'm fully seated.

A groan slips out of my mouth. "Damn, Red, you kinda lied to me."

"I did?" she asks breathlessly, moving her hips.

"You said you're wet, but you're actually dripping."

"Smart-ass."

I place my hands on her hips as she fucks me. Her eyes are closed, and more locks have fallen out of her bun. Cheeks flushed, she lets out a moan. It sends a zing of hot energy right to my dick.

Gently, I move my hands up until my palms are full of her tits. I don't tug, don't pinch, just brush my fingers over her pebbled nipples. That's what she loves, and something she still enjoys after her tits became too sensitive.

"*Kak horosho*[2]," she murmurs, placing her hands on my chest.

"Only naughty girls are fucked so good, and you've been very naughty."

"So naughty…" Eyebrows punched together, her eyes find mine. "I'm almost there…"

I grab her hips, helping her move faster. "I know, baby. Let it go."

Her movements become jerkier, faster. Eyes closed, she rides me with abandon. The fire surging through my veins tells me that my release will hit me any minute. A few more moans, groans, and whimpers escape my mouth when she pinches my nipples, and we both come. Her pussy clenches around my shaft, pulsing and throbbing. I prolong her release, helping her ride it out.

When she climbs off me and lies down on her back, we're both sweaty and breathing heavily. I turn on my side and prop my head on my hand.

"Are you comfortable?"

She smiles, cupping my face. "Yeah. Just a few minutes, and then I'll need you to help me to stand."

"Anything for you." I take her hand and press her palm to my lips. "I've spent five years around you, and I'm still in awe of how stunning

2. So good

you are. And how a girl like you would've wanted to be with a man like me."

"A man like you? Loyal to a fault, always ready to stand up for his friends and closest people? A guy who loves so deeply and so strongly that it seems like sometimes you even forget how to breathe when you look at me? A guy who is respectful, caring, and who is a perfect best friend to my husband?" She grins. "I don't know about you, but to me, this man sounds pretty awesome."

"When you put it like that..." I trail off, just to tease her. Then I take a deep breath and say, hoping it will sound right. "*Kocham cię.*[3]"

Her eyes widen. Lips parted, she gapes at me in silence. Worry creeps under my skin. What if I said it so horribly—

"You started learning Polish?" Yana breathes.

I nod.

She pulls my face down and kisses me fiercely. It's lips and tongues, even teeth when she decides to nibble on my bottom lip. When she finally leans away, breathing rapidly, she's smiling.

"You're amazing," she tells me. "I'm sure your grannie would've been proud of you. You're learning so much about her heritage, about the country she came from, about its history. And learning Polish is absolutely mindblowing."

"Obviuosly, I'm not that good with Russian as Logan, but after learning it—I decided that it's long overdue for me to finally start learning Polish. My granny Kasia would've been surprised because no matter how many times she tried to teach me—it never worked."

"She would've been proud of you. I know it." She plants a little kiss on my mouth. "And now I can even tell you '*Ya kachaju ciabie.*' It's 'I love you' in Belarusian."

"*Kocham cię bardzo*[4]," I say again before kissing her slowly. "I love you, Red."

"I love you too, Cam."

---

3. I love you
4. I love you so much

I sit on the couch with Yana between my legs, her back pressed to my chest. My hand rests on her baby bump. An occasional kick in my palm makes me think that our baby girl is going to be a soccer player. *Serendipity* is playing on the TV as we wait for Logan to come here in forty minutes, as he called us from the store.

The feeling of belonging that I never feel without Yana or Logan around heats up my skin, like the warmest hug on a windy day. It fills my whole body with the energy that makes my veins buzz. I'm relaxed and content and happy, *so damn happy*. On some days when the doubts and gloomy thoughts sneak into my brain, all this feels like a fantasy. As if for the last five years, I've been stuck in some fairy tale where my best friend and I are in love with the same girl, and she loves us just as much.

But Yana and Logan always remind me that this is real. This is our life. That there's no Yana and Camden without Logan, just like there's no Yana and Logan without me. She is ours, and we are hers. We make it work. Our relationship is full of love and mutual respect, and I wouldn't change it for anything in the world.

I'm exactly where I should be, and I'll do anything to make the girl of my dreams happy.

Me and my best friend will do anything for her.

Because...she is our queen. Our only ruler, and we will gladly serve her till the last breath.

**The End**

# Afterword

**THANK YOU SO MUCH FOR READING!**

If you enjoyed **A Very Merry Match Point**, I'd be immensely grateful if you can leave a review. Hope you fell in love with these three just like I did when I was writing it.

**HADE** is coming next! The second book in my Hale Brothers' series will be released in February, 2026. It's a very different vibe, very different story from Hunter&Piper's, and hopefully you will love Hayden&Riley's accidental pregnancy romance.

For exclusive bonus content and new releases make sure to sign up for my newsletter via my website. Follow me on my socials for news, announcements and giveaways.

## Acknowledgments

To *my husband* and *my son*, thank you for being there for me always, and for your understanding whenever I'm chasing another deadline.

To *Yana*, my friend who inspires me to be better, to be more curious, and pushes me to continue learning new things every single day. A special thank you for pushing me to start learning how to play tennis! You rock!

To *Alwyn*, there's not enough words to explain how grateful I am to you. This journey is so much better with you on it.

To my editors: *Beth, Caroline and Emily*, beyond grateful for all your hard work and for helping me make this story better.

To *Anna*, thank you for this stunning cover that matches my Sinners on the Ice SE covers perfectly! You're incredibly talented, and it's always a pleasure to work with you.

To my *PA Krissy*, and my content creators queens *Cassie* and *Kenz*, forever grateful for everything you're doing for me and my books. You're superstars!

To *my content team*, thank you so much for your love for my stories and for all the support you show me and my books.

To my amazing *readers*, thank you for reading my books and falling in love with my characters. I wouldn't be here without you.

## Also by Anastasija White

SIN-BIN: An Enemies to Lovers College Hockey Romance

BARN BURNER: A Fake Dating Hockey Romance

HALE: A Single Dad Sports Romance

BREAKAWAY: An Accidental Marriage Hockey Romance

POWER PLAY: A Second Chance Hockey Romance

Breaking Rules (Rules Duet, book 1)

Changing Rules (Rules Duet, book 2)

DEVIOUS LOVE: A Stepbrother Romance

A Very Merry Match Point

HADE: An Accidental Pregnancy Romance (2026)

# About the Author

Anastasija is an indie author who spends her days creating swoon-worthy and steamy stories that will make your heart race. Her writing is filled with flawed and relatable characters that you'll find yourself rooting for. Whether you're in the mood for angsty drama or steamy romance, her stories take you on a rollercoaster ride of emotions with guaranteed happy endings.

When she's not writing, she loves to lose herself in reading books, rewatching her favorite tv-shows and spending time with her son. She loves traveling and exploring the world, and then including places she visited in her novels.

If you're a fan of romance that leaves you breathless and begging for more, Anastasija is the author for you. Connect with her on Instagram and TikTok, where she loves to hear from her readers and share sneak peeks of her books and upcoming projects.

Printed in Dunstable, United Kingdom

75598258R00092